The Man Who Wasn't There

Chief Constable Gilliant has suggested to Chief Inspector Lyle that he apply for a detective superintendentship at Lessford. Gilliant's motive behind this is revealed to Lyle when he has secured the post: a spate of undetected, gangland killings has made Gilliant certain there is a traitor on his force.

From his first day at Lessford, Lyle realises that Gilliant's instinct is right; but the identity of the rotten apple is obscured by other corruptions and a deep distrust of the new man. The only way to the truth is for Lyle to expose himself as corrupt.

As always with John Wainwright's novels, this is not a simple whodunnit but a multi-stranded mystery which proves the dark side of human nature and its shocking capacity for evil. And the final explanation of the man who wasn't there will surprise and satisfy all readers.

THE MAN WHO WASN'T THERE

John Wainwright

MACMILLAN
LONDON

First published in Great Britain in 1989 by
MACMILLAN LONDON LIMITED
4 Little Essex Street London WC2R 3LF
and Basingstoke

Associated companies in Auckland, Delhi, Dublin,
Gaborone, Hamburg, Harare, Hong Kong, Johannesburg,
Kuala Lumpur, Lagos, Manzini, Melbourne, Mexico City,
Nairobi, New York, Singapore and Tokyo

ISBN 0-333-51132-8

A CIP catalogue record for this book is available from
the British Library.

Typeset by Matrix, 21 Russell Street, London WC2

Printed and bound in Great Britain by
The Camelot Press Ltd, Southampton

As I was going up the stair
I met a man who wasn't there.
He wasn't there again today.
I wish, I wish he'd stay away.

'The Psychoed'
by Hughes Mearns

1

I watched the large bird preening itself on the dark, slate-coloured rocks near the water's edge. I am no ornithologist, but even *I* could identify it as a cormorant. At that moment it seemed to have more reason for being around than I did. If it was delousing itself it was, at least, doing something positive.

I was into my second coffee and had just lighted my third cigarette and, if the health freaks were to be believed, I was committing slow-motion suicide. So I shortened my life, watched the cormorant and, as a sop to boredom, marvelled at the colour of the sea. Up North, on the west coast – which was my home base – the stretch between the English and Irish coasts remains a constant grey. Sometimes steel grey. Sometimes dark grey. Always *dirty* grey. But this stretch of the English Channel was aquamarine – the colour a sea *should* be – with a curving, pale-green path showing some underwater tide change.

To pass the time I tried to recall the conversation of ten days ago.

'Forgive me, chief inspector, but you seem a little old to be applying for this post.'

Gilliant had smiled polite innocence as he'd made the remark. It had been a neat piece of play-acting.

Grant, the assistant chief, had added, 'What we *don't* want is the hassle of filling this same vacancy within the next two or three years.'

'You see our problem,' Gilliant had said, gently.

The third member of the interview team hadn't spoken. He'd given the impression of being mildly bored by the whole thing.

I'd chosen my words with some care. I'd spoken directly to Gilliant.

'I'm quite fit, chief constable. Remarkably healthy for my age. I have no intention of retiring from the force – *any* force – within the foreseeable future.'

It had all been very polite, very po-faced and very formal. It had also been one elongated con.

I drew on my cigarette and watched the cormorant busy itself with the feathers under one half-raised wing. A small motor boat curled in from the left; from the direction of Whitsand Bay. The bow wave left whipped–cream–white splashes as it slapped the gentle swell. The wake seemed to arrow-head all the way out to the horizon.

To my right the hump of St George's Island looked black and forbidding across the narrow channel. It was neither of these things. It was remarkably fertile. Daffodils bloomed there weeks before they bloomed on the mainland. And it was very private. The run of the tide along that deceptively peaceful-looking channel made sure of that and, so far, the owners had refused all offers by the funfair crowd. One tiny splash of Paradise was not yet up for grabs.

I tasted my coffee. It was good coffee, but it was getting cold and I wondered how much longer I'd have to wait.

I'd known Gilliant for some years. It hadn't been a close friendship. Not, that is, until the Campbell affair.* Even then it had been the brand of friendship based on reciprocal admiration rather than common interests. Chief constables and chief inspectors don't readily mix. The gap in rank takes a little spanning. Get to superintendent and

*See *Blind Brag* by John Wainwright, also published by Macmillan.

above and, okay, everybody's in the upper echelon and the suspicion of crawling or boot-licking melts away, but until *then* . . .

Which was why I'd been surprised by his phone call some weeks before. It had been home-to-home – not office-to-office – and that, too, had surprised me.

'Are you happy in your work, Lyle?'

'I beg your pardon?'

'At Rogate-on-Sands? Do you feel like a move?'

'That all depends,' I'd fenced.

'Promotion?'

'I'll take it when it comes.' I had marked time while wondering what the hell made a man like Gilliant play coy.

'*Police Review*,' he'd said flatly.

'Not a bad journal.' The guessing game had moved on a little. 'A bit Met orientated but other than that it has its moments.'

'Buy next week's issue.'

'Something interesting?'

'There's a vacancy advertised. Detective superintendent.'

'Really?'

'Here, at Lessford.' He'd paused, then added, 'As a personal favour, apply.'

'Will it do any good?'

'We have to go through the motions, Lyle.' He'd paused again. A longer pause. Then he'd said, 'And by the way . . . we've never met. We don't even know each other.'

'And this conversation hasn't taken place?'

'Quite.'

Then he'd rung off.

That had been the start of it all. I'd applied, been short-listed, been interviewed and landed the job. Throughout the pantomime Gilliant and I had acted like strangers.

As he'd shaken my hand in congratulation he'd said,

'Welcome aboard, Mr Lyle. I think we've made a good choice.'

'Thank you, sir.'

'You'll take over the appointment on Monday, March the thirtieth. Right?'

'Yes, sir.'

'I shall be away until the following Monday.' He'd smiled. 'Enjoying a fortnight's break at my brother's place in Devon.'

'I hope the weather favours you.'

'Relaxation, Mr Lyle.' The smile had widened. 'Away from the cares of office. Assistant Chief Constable Grant will show you round, and *I'll* see you a week later.'

It had been one big put-on. The reason for it was still beyond me, but I'd played along. 'Police Politics' was a parlour game I'd horsed around with myself, but not often. Nor had my puny pulling of strings ever matched whatever Gilliant was up to.

I hadn't worried too much. The trick was (I told myself) to accept the superintendentship, then watch each hobbed pan carefully and see which lid rattled first as the steam pressure increased.

It hadn't been as easy as that.

Three days ago Gilliant had again telephoned me at my home.

'I understand you're having a break before you move to Lessford.'

The chances were he'd checked with my own DHQ.

'A few days annual leave still owing,' I'd admitted.

'Have you arranged to go somewhere?'

'No. Maybe a few early nights. Maybe a couple of lie-ins. Catch up with some reading ... that sort of thing.'

'Do you know this part of the country?' he'd asked.

'Devon? I take it that's where you're speaking from.'

'Devon. Cornwall.'

'Cornwall, a little. I don't know Devon. Why do you ask?'

'Looe? Do you know Looe?'

'I know where it is.' I'd repeated, 'Why do you ask?'

'I'd like you to meet me there.'

'Oh!'

'I'll see you're reimbursed for any out-of-pocket expenses.'

'I'd rather like to know what—'

'Monday, if it's not too inconvenient. Monday the twenty-third.'

'I can *make* it convenient,' I'd offered.

'Good. Let's say two-thirty in the afternoon. West Looe. You cross the bridge from East Looe and take the immediate left turn. Hannafore. It's signed. There's a first-rate pub-cum-restaurant on your right. Tom Sawyer's Tavern. It has a small coffee lounge overlooking the sea. That's where I'll meet you.'

'Chief constable, I think I deserve a little more—'

'The coffee lounge of Tom Sawyer's Tavern. Monday, at two-thirty.'

He'd rung off before I could push for more details and, having committed myself, I'd travelled south yesterday (Sunday) and booked in at the Punch Bowl Inn, about six miles outside Looe. I'd needed the rest. Four hundred and fifty miles, just over, mainly motorway driving, does nothing for soul or temper. Nor had the endless contraflow systems added much to the enjoyment. I'd arrived knackered, and only excellent food, a few stiff drinks and a good night's sleep in a comfortable bed had brought back near-normality.

And now I was in the coffee lounge of Tom Sawyer's Tavern, smoking cigarettes, drinking coffee, and wondering why the hell chief constables always look upon even moderate punctuality as a slur upon their virility.

11

The waitress moved smoothly into the lounge to collect the cup, empty the ashtray and wipe down an already spotless table. She'd obviously been sent to see what the deuce I was up to.

'I have an appointment, and he's late.' Some sort of explanation seemed necessary.

'That's quite all right, sir.'

'I'll have another coffee while I wait, please.'

'Yes, sir.'

A Rover pulled into the car park across the road from the lounge, and I added, 'Make that two coffees, miss. My friend seems to have arrived at last.'

2

Gilliant shook hands and apologised for being late.

'This damn county. It's one huge traffic bottleneck, in or out of season. It's worse than Devon.'

'At least it's a nice day.'

'Quite.'

'I've ordered two coffees.'

'Good.'

We sat down at the table and he fished in his pockets, then offered me an opened packet of cigarettes. As I took one I remembered something somebody had once mentioned – I forget who, but somebody *had* mentioned it – that Gilliant rarely smoked. Only when he was worried. He was smoking now, and the proffered twenty pack was half empty.

We smoked. We sipped coffee. We talked trivialities and he seemed to be sizing me up; finalising some decision he'd already reached. His eyes were slightly narrowed

12

and he watched my face more than was necessary. When he wasn't speaking his lips were a shade tighter than they need have been at the corners.

I, in turn, viewed him from a new angle. He was the man shortly to become my new chief constable.

A tall man, he topped the six foot mark by a couple of inches. He was slim, as opposed to my own knuckle-boned gauntness. His hair was iron-grey, brushed back and with white wings above each ear. He was a remarkably good-looking guy for his age.

I knew him to be another thing, too. He was a copper's copper . . . and there aren't many of those around these days.

'Cornwall,' he was saying, and his voice was deep and quiet, with the hint of a drawl. He was gazing out along the coast. 'A county with more than its fair share of eccentrics and artists.'

'And smugglers,' I smiled.

'Restless.' He murmured the word, as if to himself. 'The natives are too near the sea for prolonged tranquillity.'

'Rogate is tranquil enough,' I reminded him.

'Ah, but no rocks. No hidden hazards.'

Gilliant had that faraway look I'd come to recognise in the older hands. It went with a nostalgia for the once-upon-a-time. A time when the upper ranks weren't stiff with career coppers; with men who know the book, know when to smile and know which wine to order at flash meals; who keep their buttons shiny and their trousers creased and can come up with a dozen reasons why crime statistics nudge the ionosphere . . . and not one reason linked to lousy policing.

He stared at me for a moment, then asked, 'Do you think you'll miss Rogate-on-Sands?'

'I have no friends.' I hoped it answered his question.

He looked mildly surprised.

13

'Acquaintances,' I explained. 'Colleagues with whom I happily work. But, no *friends*.'

'And not even married,' he smiled.

'Married,' I contradicted, gently. He was obviously probing and I saw no reason why he should be denied the truth. 'Married some number of years ago . . . then divorced. It's on my records. When you get them, you'll be able to check.'

'I – er – I wasn't . . .'

'Forgive me, chief constable, but I think you *were*. There's nothing to hide. Married. No children . . . fortunately. It lasted three years, then she saw sense.'

'Sense?'

'Realised it wouldn't work. I'm not the marrying kind.' I tasted my coffee. 'The last I heard, she was in America. Remarried. I hope she's happy. With the right man, she will be.'

'Oh!'

'Nor,' I ended, 'have I homosexual tendencies.'

'You're rather an unusual character, Mr Lyle,' he said softly.

'I'm a policeman.' It seemed time to put the cards on the table, face upwards. 'In the final analysis, that's *all* I am. But even *that* is something.'

'To be telephoned by a chief constable – a man with whom I've worked, but a man I hardly know – and to be asked to apply for a detective superintendentship in his force. A little strange, wouldn't you say? Unusual? That, at the very least. Flattering, I suppose. But I'm not susceptible to flattery. "Going through the motions." That's the phrase you used, Mr Gilliant. It was a fiddle, and we both knew it. Unless I'm very much mistaken, the other two at the final interview *didn't* know it.'

'Go on.' Gilliant drew deeply on his cigarette.

'This meeting,' I continued. '*Not* part of the fiddle. And yet, a face-to-face meeting, almost five hundred miles from our respective force headquarters. Slightly "inconvenient" . . . for both of us. Curiosity brought me here, Mr Gilliant. I was intrigued. I'm *still* intrigued. *You*, on the other hand, are now the one who is curious. Undecided. Worried. Have you made the right choice? Have I some weakness you know nothing about? Those are the questions you're still asking yourself. I think, for your own peace of mind, you should answer them. Or, if you like, ask *me* . . . and *I'll* answer them.'

He nodded, slowly, and his eyes never left my face.

'I think,' he said, 'I made the right decision. Perhaps even a very *wise* decision.' He screwed what was left of his cigarette into the glass ashtray and stood up. 'I think we'll stroll along the coast road, Mr Lyle.'

3

By comparison with the weather I'd left at Rogate-on-Sands it was almost spring-like. Marine Drive was a coast road; a wide and pleasant cul-de-sac which ended where the South West Peninsula Coast Path took over. We walked slowly along the seaward side of the road, reached the gate, turned, retraced our steps until we'd passed the parked cars, then turned and, again, walked towards the gate.

Gilliant talked. I listened.

'Three murders in the last nine months. Three . . . maybe four. All undetected. Officially, two men and one woman. No great loss to the community, in that they were all three part of the Lessford gangland crowd. But that isn't the point. The point – the only point that matters – is that they were *murders*. Three major crimes. All undetected.

15

I don't give a damn about statistics, Lyle. Statistics can be handled . . . excused. But I *do* give a damn about the gut feeling I have. That certain people in Lessford count themselves above the law. I've seen too many murders to have much doubt. These were "enforcer" killings.

'Your predecessor, Calladine – Detective Superintendent Calladine – held the same view. He died, little more than a month ago. A hit-and-run accident . . . on the face of things. In the early hours of the morning, while he was walking home. Motor Manslaughter? I think not, Mr Lyle. Nor a 'Drunk in Charge'. I think it was a deliberate run-down. I think he, too, was murdered.'

He paused and waited for a reaction. When he didn't get a reaction he pushed his hands into the pockets of his army twill trousers and continued his story as we walked.

'It didn't shock me. I had enough police time behind me *not* to be shocked. But, it was no bedtime tale. Three quick, "back-alley" killings. The men knifed from behind. Obviously by an expert.

'Just the one blow. Probably with the neck held in the crook of the left arm. They showed a certain murderous artistry. A technique taught to commandos – taught to the SAS types – used by the élite killers of the world.

'The woman strangled. Again, from behind. Again, swiftly and by somebody very knowledgeable in the art.

'The boffins gave their opinion. They reported, "Something in the nature of cheese wire". Cheese wire. Piano wire. Nylon fishing line. The bloody string from a yo-yo. Who the hell cares? Whoever did it knew his business. No sound. No struggle. Just like *that*!' He took a hand from its pocket long enough to snap his fingers. 'No mistakes. The work of an expert.

'Nothing had been stolen from the bodies. The woman's clothes hadn't been disturbed. No known jealousies, no known quarrels, no obvious motives.

'At each killing the police machine had slipped into top gear. Mobile Incident Caravans. Posters asking for information. A special telephone number and guaranteed anonymity. Every jack at every level had leaned on snouts and informers. Every scrap of information had been fed into a computer. At each murder the background of the victim had been fine-tooth-combed for some hint as to who might be responsible.

'Nothing!

'From the first we knew this was no family-quarrel-kitchen-knife situation. Both men were hoodlums. The violent death of either wouldn't have surprised anybody. But it was deeper than that . . . both times. More involved than GBH gone too far. The same with the woman. She was a moll. The odds were against her living to a ripe old age. But – again – it wasn't *so* easy. There was another dimension. We reached *that* conclusion at the first killing. It was a "message". They all were. *From* whom? *To* whom? We still don't know.'

We leaned on the gate beyond which was the footpath and, this time, I opened the cigarette packet.

Gilliant exhaled cigarette smoke and sighed, 'Sugden went mad.'

'Sugden?' I asked my first question.

'Sugden. Assistant Chief Constable (Crime). You haven't met him. You've met Grant, the Assistant Chief Constable (Admin.). He was there at the final interview. So was Harris – ACC (Crime) for the Bordfield Area.'

'The very bored gentleman?'

'He was standing in for Sugden. Sugden was having a few days off duty. He needed them.'

'Tell me about Calladine,' I suggested.

We strolled back towards the cars and the more Gilliant talked the less I understood about the late Detective Superintendent Calladine.

Listening to the spaces between the words I reached

my own conclusions. In a world where men are naturally close-mouthed, Calladine had been a very secretive type. He'd been the sort of clown capable of making two and two add up to a neat four, but who'd guyed his colleagues into believing the total to be only three and a half.

'He did things his own way,' explained Gilliant.

'Meaning he liked to be a one-man band.'

'We all have our faults, Lyle.'

'Quite. But, as the actress said to the bishop . . . some are bigger than others.'

Friend Calladine was dead and buried, and one must not speak ill of the dead, but I doubt if he and I would have ever been bosom pals.

Nevertheless, he'd been Sugden's buddy, and Sugden had hand-picked him as a man capable of stitching the three killings together. To make the various parts of the jigsaw fit. To retrace the steps along a score of blind alleys, check that they *were* blind alleys and, if so, *why* they were blind alleys.

'I think he was getting somewhere,' said Gilliant.

'If only six foot under,' I murmured sourly.

Gilliant talked a little more. I listened, but I'd already formed certain opinions. He left the clincher till we were back at the cars and I was resting my backside against the hood of my own Cortina.

'We had a council of war, two days before Calladine was killed. Just Sugden, Calladine and myself. It was a very private meeting, and certain conclusions were reached.'

'And?' I asked.

'There's a rotten apple in the barrel.'

'There's a rotten apple in *every* barrel.'

The remark meant damn-all. It was one of those smart remarks which tend to encourage specifics.

The muscles around his jaw hardened a little as he said, 'The blind alleys were blind alleys because somebody on *our* side was feeding the bastards information.

It didn't matter which way we moved, we were blocked. Every raid . . . they knew we were coming. Every time we pulled somebody in for questioning . . . a solicitor was there within fifteen minutes.'

'They're entitled to a solicitor,' I reminded him.

'They didn't have to *send* for the damn solicitor,' he growled. 'He just arrived.'

'Forensic fun and games,' I smiled.

'It's not funny, Lyle.'

I took the smile away and waited.

'It happens, sometimes.' Gilliant sighed the words as if he was telling me some as-yet-undisclosed secret. 'It shouldn't but it *does*. Every copper isn't as white as driven snow.'

'Or even driven slush.'

'There's a strong possibility that's why Calladine was killed.'

'If he was getting too close,' I agreed.

'He *was* getting close.'

The thought struck me that I was inheriting a dead man's chair. If Gilliant was right, he was dead because he'd been touching some raw nerves and, obviously, Gilliant wanted me to take over where Calladine had left off. Quite suddenly this superintendentship I'd accepted had nasty edges.

Gilliant frowned a faraway stare across Looe Bay and towards a clear-cut horizon. He, too, was a very worried man.

'Your own force,' I suggested. 'Internal Affairs. Why not let *them* sniff around a bit?'

'Coppers,' he muttered. 'Lessford coppers. Lessford *detectives*. Who the hell do you trust in a situation like this?'

'Get an outside force in. Get a—'

'That's what I *have* done.'

'Eh?'

'In effect. *You.*'

'Oh!'

'I know what you mean, Lyle.' He turned his head and looked at me to give emphasis to his words. 'Lessford is a big force. *Too* big. One man – one chief constable – can't be everywhere. He can't know everything. Remember Operation Countryman? To clean up the Met. To uncover the bribes. To shift the corruption.

'It got nowhere . . . because the Met was too big. Files were "lost". Telephones "broke down". Men required for interview were suddenly "not available". They ran rings round us and we didn't even know who "they" were. Not the men at the top. We were sure of that. Not at the *very* top. But some weren't too far down the ladder. And others, of course. All the way down the line. They knew who we were. They knew why we were there. They could have played puss-in-the-corner till doom cracked. They could have. They *would* have.'

He stopped speaking for a moment, then there was a blind determination in his voice as he continued, 'It's not going to happen at Lessford. Once around *those* particular houses is enough for me. This time they're going to be investigated without *knowing* they're being investigated. Just you, and me – and Sugden.'

4

I moved on to the M5 north of Okehampton and from there it was the usual dreary game of catch-me-if-you-can with lorries speeding up towards Bristol and Birmingham. At some time during the night it had started to rain, a steady, misty downpour, and we were back to true March weather. The brown spray thrown up by the rear wheels plastered itself across the windscreen and the wipers cleared a double arc through which I had to peer. The periodic contraflows didn't help. The damn motorway system! It was forever in need of repair. We could put men on the moon. We'd just about solved the mystery of creation. But we couldn't yet build a road capable of taking the weight of modern traffic.

After the first hundred miles the concentration brought a dull ache to the nape of my neck and I watched for a sign showing a service area.

Gilliant hadn't been pleased, but the hell with Gilliant. *He'd* come to *me* (not the other way round) and if he wanted me he could have me . . . but on *my* terms.

I'd said, 'And, if what happened to Calladine happens to me?'

'Why should it?' He'd looked quite startled at the suggestion.

'Why *shouldn't* it?' I'd countered. 'My ribs are no more reinforced than Calladine's were.'

'You'll be a stranger. An unknown quantity.'

'Not for long. Not if I turn over stones and find some creepy-crawlies.'

'You'll be answerable only to me.'

'Chief constable . . .' My sigh had been deep and a little hammy. 'That I'm responsible only to *you* won't give much comfort when I'm bleeding to death in the gutter of some deserted road.'

'You disappoint me, Lyle.'

'Indeed?'

'I thought you were a man who didn't scare easily.'

'Whoever told you that was pulling your leg.' I'd matched him, taunt for taunt. 'I scare very easily. That's why I'm still around.'

'All right. What else do you want?'

'Back-up,' I'd said bluntly. 'I want somebody alongside me I can trust.'

'You'll have Sugden.'

'I don't *know* Sugden.'

'He's one of the best men in the—'

'Whereas, those you're asking me to nail *do* know Sugden.'

'You can trust him.' His voice had become tight and hard. 'Of all the police officers I've ever—'

'Oh, no.' I'd shaken my head slowly but firmly. I'd had him over a barrel and I'd enjoyed the slight feeling of temporary superiority. 'This is a very messy baby, chief constable. Add to that the fact that you're approaching it from an uncommonly devious angle. What you're after may not be impossible, but it's not going to be *easy*. However, if Sugden is so bloody good, let *Sugden* have a swing at it . . . and *I'll* watch.' He hadn't answered, and I'd continued, 'If *I* do it, I want somebody inside.'

'Meaning?'

'Inside,' I'd repeated. 'Somebody inside *their* ranks, playing *their* game for *my* benefit.'

'It's a good angle . . . but, I don't see *how*.'

'The Chief Constables' Mutual Assistance Society.' I'd allowed myself a quick, sardonic smile at the impudence of what I was going to ask. 'Contact my chief constable – my *present* chief constable – and request off-the-record assistance. Don't tell him why. Don't tell him *anything*. As a favour, put it any way you like, ask him to put one of his detective inspectors on Duty Elsewhere detail until further notice. Detective Inspector Faber. The ideal situation would be for him to be put on Duty Elsewhere immediately, tell him nothing and let *me* brief him tomorrow. Then, even *you* won't know what he looks like.'

'Tomorrow!'

'It gets him into Lessford before *I* arrive.'

'Good God! And you call *me* devious.'

'Chief constable, if I trot along dragging a complete stranger in my wake it might look obvious.'

'Oh, I approve.' He hadn't sounded too sure as he'd added, 'I just don't know whether your chief constable will agree to the idea.'

'Not if *I* asked him, but . . .' I'd moved my shoulders. '*He* might want a favour, one day.'

'There's a limit to how much influence I have,' he'd warned.

'Nobody knows, until they try.'

But I'd known, and I knew now. I eased the Cortina into the slow lane, caught the full force of rear-wheel spray from an articulated vehicle and leaned forward to see the mouth of the service area slip road. *I* knew. I knew Galliant was no run-of-the-mill chief constable. He had friends in high places. Junior ministers and above periodically sought his advice. More than that. He was on buddy-buddy terms with members of the Whitehall crowd. People with *real* pull.

Which was why I hadn't been surprised when he'd telephoned, before I set off north. Things had already been fixed. Faber had already been taken off the streets. He'd been told to wait for further instructions. And that was *all* he'd been told.

Meanwhile, despite the lack of signs, I found the service area car park. I left the Cortina, made my way through a fruit-machine-infested hall and, eventually, reached the food.

The heavy-goods boys were busy stuffing themselves with mid-morning sustenance. Fried eggs, fried bacon, fried bread and fried tomatoes. Nevertheless, the old 'greasy spoon' image of these places had long gone. Neat little alcoves with neat little tables jig-sawed around the floor space and, if they looked a mite incongruous peopled by muscled men with pot bellies and tattooed forearms, it

23

made a pleasant change from the chips-with-everything set-up of the old days.

Up-to-the-minute gimcrackery was catered for by smoking and non-smoking areas, but that was a gag. With partitions only shoulder-high when you were seated everybody breathed in tobacco smoke.

I collected tea and Cellophane-wrapped sandwiches from the counter, found an empty table, chewed, sipped tea and smoked while I pondered upon what I'd let myself in for.

For example, Lessford. Or, to give it its full style and title, Lessford Metropolitan Police District.

Some few years ago a Home Office clown with time on his hands had drawn a line on a map. At a guess it must have been a cheap school atlas because the line enclosed two cities – Lessford and Bordfield – each with its own force and a damn great chunk of surrounding county constabulary. More than a million and a half acres, inhabited by three million, plus, citizens and policed by just over seven thousand coppers. That was the size of the bundle Gilliant had had dropped in his lap.

Lesser men would have made for the hills. Gilliant did what he could to make the thing manageable. Two 'regions'. In the north Bordfield Region, in the south Lessford Region; each with its regional headquarters, each with its own ACC (Crime) and its own ACC (Admin). In effect, twin forces with a single chief constable and a single force headquarters at Lessford.

It was one hell of a big pie, and it held one hell of a lot of potatoes. One – maybe more than one – of those potatoes had gone rotten and my job was going to be that of potato-grubber until I'd found it. Or *them*.

It made the Rubik Cube look like noughts and crosses.

I screwed what was left of my cigarette into the ashtray, drained the fast-cooling tea and walked from the eating area. I called at the shop off the foyer to buy barley-sugar

24

sweets and to get some change, then I claimed one of the telephones in one corner of the hall and dialled Faber's home number.

5

The Tickled Trout is one of those hotels-cum-restaurants Egon Ronay has missed. The regulars don't mind, because the regulars figure themselves to be on to a good thing and aren't too keen on chinless wonders on their way north screwing things up by arriving in large lumps and spoiling the quiet and very select atmosphere.

It is just off the M6 junction with the A59, and I'd ordered dinner for two for eight o'clock. I arrived at just after seven-thirty, having called at home for a shower and a change of clothes, and Faber was standing at the bar as I strolled into the lounge.

He ordered a second whisky and water and, as I joined him, he said, 'Your word seems to be my command, Lyle. What the hell goes on?'

'Over dinner,' I promised. 'There's a very private corner. I've made sure it's reserved for us.'

'You have pull too.'

'You'd be surprised,' I smiled. 'Get used to the feeling. You're going to *be* surprised.'

'Lessford?' he fished.

'You'll be told.'

'You land a top-ranker's office there and suddenly *I'm* nudged into the shadows. All highly mysterious, until you arrange this meeting. I don't have to be a Holmes – or even a Watson – to put those two bricks together. The answer is not a lemon. The answer is Lessford.'

'The first rule of good detective work,' I said airily. 'Keep your eyes open and your mouth shut.'

'Is that advice, or a warning?'

'Both.'

'With rank attached?'

'I could make it *that* too.'

'And not for one moment do I think you wouldn't.'

This was the man. This was Faber. I didn't like him, but I hadn't chosen him on the basis of personal popularity. I'd chosen him because he didn't look like a copper, he didn't act like a copper and he didn't talk like a copper. More than that, he was a very cunning copper. He'd made detective inspector because he had the God-given knack of always keeping one step ahead of trouble. That, and a memory like a sponge.

The head waiter eased his way towards us and handed each of us a menu.

I asked Faber, 'You like rainbow trout?'

'Are you paying?'

'Of course.'

'In that case, I like rainbow trout.'

'With the trimmings,' I ordered. I glanced at the menu again, and added, 'For me, a salad. Just an evening snack. I'll let the wine waiter choose what we have to drink.'

'Yes, sir. Fifteen minutes?'

'Fine.'

As the waiter left earshot Faber said, 'Whatever it is, it's got between you and your appetite.'

'You're jumping to conclusions, friend.' I smiled. 'My guts are already filled with motorway stodge.'

'North or south?'

'You're asking questions again,' I warned.

He shrugged and the accompanying grin was more than a little sour. He'd tried. That could always be said about Faber – he persevered to the point of being a damn nuisance. And that was *another* thing I was counting on.

Fifteen minutes later we were eating.

The food was excellent, the wine was good and the

privacy was absolute. I toyed with my salad and hoped what I was saying wasn't spoiling Faber's trout. In fairness, he listened without interruption and when I ended he dabbed his lips with his napkin before he expressed an opinion.

'You've lost what few marbles you had left, Lyle.'

'Meaning?'

'It won't work.'

'They've said that about so many things.' I kept cool. His initial reaction had been what I'd expected. 'They said it about heavier-than-air flying machines. Splitting the atom. Heart transplants. So many things.'

'Jesus Christ! You're talking about conning professional con men.'

'Slobs,' I contradicted. 'Gangsters. High-class tearaways. It takes neither brains nor skill to put the frighteners on.'

'They're not mugs.'

'They're mugs,' I insisted. 'They have brawn, but very little brain. They're on top of the world. Think about it, Faber. Think about it from their point of view. Three killings . . . and nobody's seen the inside of a police cell. If Gilliant is right, they've knocked over a copper – a detective superintendent, no less – and walked away from *that*.' I waved my fork to emphasise what I was saying. 'These bastards are all the same. From Capone to the Krays. They're lucky, maybe lucky for a long time, and, in time, they think they can't lose. They think they're fireproof.'

'They have a man inside the force,' argued Faber. 'Maybe more than one. They're getting all the griff they need. With that backing they *are* fireproof.'

'And we leave it?' I mocked.

'I'm not a dedicated little policeman.' The bow of his lips killed any hope I might have of taunting him into working with me. 'I feel collars because I'm *paid* to feel collars. That's all. It's no crusade, Lyle. Lessford has an infestation of mobsters. I, personally, won't lose a wink of sleep if the place runs rotten with hoodlums, tearaways or any other scum you care to mention. Lessford is not my concern. Lessford is not—'

'It is now,' I cut in coldly.

'Lyle, I am *not* a Lessford copper.'

'Oh, yes,' I nodded. 'That you are, my smart-arse little friend. As from the moment you moved to Duty Elsewhere, you were seconded to Lessford, until further notice.'

'That – that can't be done!'

'Funny man,' I sneered.

'If you think—'

'I don't think, Faber. I *know*. Check with the muscle-men who manned various picket lines in the past. We bussed men in from all points of the compass . . . remember? If we can second them by the hundred, we can second them individually.'

He digested the truth for a moment. It almost choked him, but he was wise enough to accept defeat, albeit without much grace.

Then, in a hard, unfriendly tone, he asked, 'Why me? Why specifically *me*?'

'Because you're a wild man,' I said bluntly. 'Because acting the part of a crook won't be too difficult – not for you. You might get your earhole punched. If you're lucky, that's all that will happen. You'll take it, if only to uphold your self image as a hard man.' I stared at him in silence for a moment, then continued, 'I don't like you, Faber, but nobody who knows you can accuse you of not having bottle. That's all I need. I'll do the conniving. All you have to do is obey orders . . . and that you *will* do. Be advised, therefore. Listen to what I'm going to tell you. Listen very carefully and, for the first time in your life, obey instructions to the letter. You'll convince them,

28

Faber. You'd *better* convince them. They're cop killers . . . or think they are. So, if you *don't* convince them, they just might feel inclined to do a repeat performance. And a warning. Any two-timing on your part – any hints dropped as to who, or what you are, or who, or what you might be – and *I* move into action. I feed them enough back-door information to make sure you end up dog's meat. And – I promise – I'll happily stand back and watch them tear your throat out.'

He breathed, 'You bastard. You utter, unmitigated bastard,' and I didn't blame him. In his position, I'd have reached the same conclusion.

I snapped, 'You'd better believe that, Faber. You'd better never forget it. Now, having been allowed to express the only opinion you're *going* to express, listen very carefully.'

6

I shed no tears as I drove back to Rogate-on-Sands. My assessment of Faber hadn't been far out. He couldn't be appealed to as a copper. He couldn't be mocked into taking on the job. The only thing left was a combination of fear and fury – and that had done the trick.

Sure, he hated my guts, but to me that was no price to pay. He'd do what he had to do *because* he hated my guts, and that, too, was okay.

Psychology?

That is its fancy name; the name they hang on it when the couch boys prod and pry into dark corners of the subconscious. But every working jack develops the ability to spot weaknesses in his fellows. He learns how to play-act any and every emotion which takes advantage of those weaknesses.

That's all I'd done with Faber. I'd goaded him, slammed rank at him and, eventually, blinded him with his own hatred.

As of now, he'd work his nuts off proving he could do what I'd suggested without even breaking into a sweat. He'd make no mistakes, because mistakes would make *him* look stupid and, for the moment, his aim in life was to make *me* look stupid.

7

The men I'd met at Lessford Police Headquarters hadn't been too surprised to see me. I was due to start there tomorrow, and it was not unnatural that an evening-before-the-event reconnoitre had seemed called for.

In fact, I'd been at Lessford most of the day.

As a city it was like most other cities. Only a poet would have claimed that it had a soul – and a pretty lousy poet, at that. It had no gender. It was neither male nor female. It was a city; a sprawling mass of a little good, a lot of bad, but mostly very mediocre architecture; a few hundred miles of roads, streets and avenues. It hadn't been planned, and that, too, showed. Like Topsy, it had just 'grow'd'. Ugly in some parts. Moderately elegant in others.

The people had the zombie look of all city dwellers. The folks I was leaving at Rogate could (I knew) look sad, look horrified, look frightened . . . anything. But always with animation in their eyes. Not so the Lessfordites. They all seemed to carry the look – the curse – of absolute defeat.

I'd seen that look in Leeds. I'd seen it in Birmingham. I'd seen it in London. Always it reminds me of the Wandering Sickness of Wells's *The Shape of Things to Come*. And it was there on the streets of Lessford.

Like every city – like every town – Lessford had its bad quarter. Its anus from which came much of the evil I would be up against. In Lessford it was North End. North End Division, where a legend called Sullivan had once waged a very personal war against mobsters and tearaways. Sullivan wasn't there any more, but that wasn't important. The crowd I'd been brought in to combat no longer lived in North End. They'd moved out to the posh division. To Park View Division. Over the years, in the mêlée of big city outlawry, the big rats had devoured the smaller rats and, having become fat and prosperous, the main rodents now nested in all-mod-con mini mansions, surrounded by well-trimmed beech hedges. They employed gardeners to keep their lawns immaculate and their flowerbeds weed free. They employed live-in help in order that their flash, common-law wives didn't have to risk cracked fingernails.

They paid good wages. And why not? There was plenty more where *that* came from.

From Park View Division they controlled the city in general and North End Division in particular.

I'd already visited North End and Park View. I had the overall picture of my coming battleground. It was depressing, and I was suitably depressed as I made my way along the pavements of the city centre.

Some few days before I'd questioned one of the Rogate snouts. A man who'd rubbed shoulders with villains he'd shared cells with in the past. A man who 'knew things'.

'You won't find many worse outside the Smoke, Mr Lyle.'

'They play rough?'

'They pull the strings, Mr Lyle. Strings as thick as bloody bell ropes.'

31

'Many of them?'

'Adams. He's the big man. Foster Adams.'

'Foster Adams?'

'He's a bloody animal, Mr Lyle. "Sweet F.A." That's what they call him – behind his back. Nobody moves in Lessford without his say-so.'

'Where does he work from?'

'Anywhere. His home – a bloody great place out Park View way. His car – car telephone, that sort of thing. And he has an office at this nightclub joint he runs. The Blue Boar. Gambling. Girlie-girlie shows. Just about anything you want . . . if you can pay for it. They tell me it's very hot, Mr Lyle.'

There'd been more, along the same lines and, even counting the normal exaggeration indulged in by every informer I'd ever met, this creep Foster Adams was obviously one of the big wheels in the Lessford criminal set-up.

I stood with my hands in the pockets of my opened raglan mac and eyed the strip lighting above and around the entrance of the Blue Boar. It was impressive, if you like expensive crap. The name was spelled out in puke-yellow, underlined in watered-down red. The boar's head motif blazed out in royal blue and the tusks deliberately hinted at twin rampant male organs of reproduction. Glass-fronted showcases on each side of the door showed the usual heavily buttocked, big-breasted females in various poses, with ostrich feathers and sequins adding schmaltz glamour to soft porn.

It was a strip joint. No better, no worse, than a thousand and one other strip joints and, like most of them, it was in a side street off one of the main thoroughfares of the city centre.

I removed a hand from its pocket and glanced at my watch. The time was less than a minute to six-thirty. The Blue Boar did not start business until eight, so I returned the hand to its pocket and continued to stare at the flash surround of a dump I knew I would eventually have to visit.

The background traffic noise from the main road masked any sound he might have made, therefore I was unprepared. The first I knew was when my mac was grabbed at the neck, from the rear, dragged down to the waist and used as a make-shift pinion for my arms. Then I was hauled off balance and swung around until the side of my head smacked against the concrete of a goose-necked lamp-standard.

Thereafter, and for a few moments . . . nothing.

I awoke to find a dumb-bell with bad breath leaning over me and working to unfasten my tie.

'It's all right, mister. There's an ambulance on its way.'

'Forget it,' I snarled.

I pushed myself upright, brushed the good Samaritan aside and steadied myself by hanging on to the lamp-standard.

'You shouldn't be standing up.'

'Forget it,' I repeated.

'I know what I'm talking about. I'm a First Aid expert.'

'I don't give a damn if you're Doctor Kildare.' I patted my breast pocket. 'Some bastard has made off with my wallet.'

The small group of gawpers looked appropriately out-raged. *Then* the flatfoot arrived and took over.

I was in no sweet temper. My head throbbed like a runaway trip-hammer, there was a gash above my eye which sent blood pouring down the front of my coat and shirt and the First Aid prat was becoming something of a nuisance.

The copper was one of the seen-it-all-done-it-all types. Sympathy and understanding were not part of his brief. His main and immediate concern was to shoo the onlookers on their way in order to prevent what he was pleased to call an 'obstruction'. I was the clown responsible for this potential 'obstruction' – and, as far as *he* was concerned, that made me an unnecessary pain in his personal rump.

The ambulance arrived, complete with siren and burning tyre rubber. I was loaded on to a stretcher and manhandled on to one of the racks. His Imperial Nibs in the size elevens followed me aboard and as the ambulance took off he settled down, opened his notebook, untopped his ballpoint and set himself up for one of the minor shocks of his life.

'Now then. I'd better have your name.'

'You'd better have my name,' I agreed.

'What is it, then?'

'Lyle.'

'Lyle? How do you spell it?'

'L-Y-L-E. Lyle.'

'Do you have any first names?'

'Certainly.' I allowed the pause to stretch itself a little. 'Detective Superintendent.'

'Eh?' His head jerked as if on a parachute elastic.

'Detective Superintendent Lyle. And now, my wooden-top friend, write the following in that notebook of yours.' I held a wad of cotton wool against my bleeding head and ignored the shushing of the ambulance attendant who was obviously well out of his usual league. I spoke at slow dictation speed. 'You will write, "I attended the scene of a mugging. I gave no assistance whatever to the injured person. I have yet to ask him whether he has had anything stolen. I have yet to ask him for a description of his attacker. I am carrying a personal radio, but I have yet to notify anybody about details of this incident." Got that?' I asked.

He finished writing then nodded, very sulkily.

'Fine.' I held out my free hand. 'Time it, date it and I'll sign it.'

'Sir, I'll—'

'Time it, date it and I'll sign it,' I repeated. 'Include

it in the report you submit, and submit that report to *me* – personally. Include in the report that I've had my wallet stolen, and that the wallet contained my bank credit card, my warrant card and about fifty pounds in Bank of England notes.'

'Sir, if I've done anything—'

'Submit the report to *me*, at Lessford Police Headquarters. I'll second-minute it, with my own observations before it goes to the chief constable.'

'Sir.' The words almost choked him. 'I'm sorry.'

'No.' I shook my head and wished to hell I hadn't. 'You're not sorry. You're frightened. But you're *going* to be sorry.'

8

The medic at the infirmary had visions of me being admitted for 'observation'. There was much high-octane language about concussion and possible minor brain damage – but that was okay, the guy was doing and saying what the Health Service was paying him to do and say. I, on the other hand, was doing what *I* was paid to do, and no quack was going to screw the lid down on my efforts.

Eventually we reached a compromise. I made do with four stitches and a blinding headache while the duty medic had to be satisfied with an outraged departure into the bowels of the massive city infirmary.

9

I was made detective superintendent the next day, Monday, March the thirtieth. Nobody hired a brass band, nobody hung out any flags and nobody did hand-stands. It was merely a new and larger force and a new and larger office.

I still carried a headache but, instead of throbbing, it was a dull curtain of pain down the left side of my face. There was also a neat technicolour effect where the tints ranged from deep red, through puce to dark blue. For the first time in years I had a real shiner.

As I climbed from the car and walked towards the shallow steps leading to the entrance of the headquarters building a small group of local newshounds moved in. I gave non-answers to the usual non-questions and cameras were aimed in my direction.

Sugden must have witnessed my arrival from the window of his office, and Sugden did nothing to hide his annoyance.

As I was later to learn, Sugden was the sort of senior policeman who counts a state of perpetual annoyance as a vital part of his duty.

I'd dumped my briefcase on the table-desk and was hanging my mac on the coatstand when he marched into the office, without even a token tap on the door.

'I'm Sugden,' he growled.

I held out my hand, but he didn't even see it.

'You,' he continued, 'are the first senior copper I've

36

known to take up a new post looking like something rescued from a concrete mixer.'

'Let's say I bruise easily,' I suggested.

'Let's say you're a prat,' he snapped. 'Mugged and robbed, the day before you take up a position of responsibility in a new force.'

'I didn't approve of Pearl Harbour, either,' I murmured.

'Eh?' he gawped at me.

'I prefer war to be declared.'

'What the hell is that supposed to—?'

'Sugden,' I said coldly. 'Eventually you may not like me. Eventually you may even hate my guts. But *know* me first. Have something upon which to base an opinion. Otherwise, that makes *you* a bloody fool.'

It stopped him. It was *meant* to stop him. Maybe he'd never been called a bloody fool before. If not, it was time somebody broke the news.

I was on safe ground. He out-ranked me by at least two strides, but I'd just arrived. Nobody was going to organise a farewell party within minutes of me walking into my nice new office.

For a moment he seemed to choke. Then he swallowed whatever was stuck in his throat and managed the ghost of a nod.

'You're taking Calladine's place,' he grunted.

'And he was your buddy?'

He didn't answer, but his nostrils widened a little.

'We'll take it as read that I'm never going to be as good as *he* was.'

'I didn't say that.' It was a reluctant capitulation.

'My top priority,' I said, 'is to find out who killed him.'

'Motor Manslaughter,' he muttered.

'At least that.'

'I wish you luck.'

'Thanks.'

He turned to leave the office, paused, then said, 'If

you're free. Eleven-thirty . . . thereabouts. There's a café. Leave here by the front entrance, turn left then first turning left. It's called the Copper Saucepan. They serve good midday snacks at a reasonable price. Better than the goo they serve at the canteen. I use it. There's a corner table reserved for me. I'll ask them to put an extra chair in place.'

He even closed the door without banging it.

It was a victory. Men like Sugden never apologise. It goes against some obscure religious belief they seem to hold. But, I'd quietened him – I'd made him back off a little – and *that* was a victory.

10

A crime file – specifically, a murder file – is always a great wodge of paper upon which is typed or written acres of useless rubbish and a few square inches of useful information. By ten o'clock I had three murder files on the desk in front of me and, one at a time, I was sorting the wheat from the chaff.

I ignored the photographs. A stiff is a stiff and he (or she) is no more dead in glossy black and white than when the hospital quack jots DOA on his official report. Equally, I skipped past the findings of the pathologist. The morgue boys know their job. They should. They handle entrails almost as often as a croupier handles gambling chips.

Two knifings, one strangulation.

Knifing Number One. Location: Gordon Court. Name of victim: Charles Barnes, also known as 'Chuck' Barnes.

In life, Barnes had been a nutcase. Convictions at

Derby, Nottingham, Rotherham, Stockport and Huddersfield, etc., etc. Barnes had been a congenital thief, but not a good thief. Good thieves don't get caught. An occasional GBH showed that, with enough encouragement, Barnes had been capable of turning nasty. He'd nicked motor cars, he'd received stolen watches, he'd tried his hand at housebreaking, he'd even forged a few cheques.

His 'arresting officers' had ranged in rank from detective inspector down to detective constable. At Lessford he'd been arrested three times. Once by Detective Sergeant Wilkins. Twice by Detective Sergeant Dooley.

Knifing Number Two. Location: Carmile Street. Name of victim: Joseph Henry Keanan.

Keanan had been more of a smoothie than Barnes. His previous convictions didn't take up as many lines and with never a hint of violence. His stamping ground had been at Lessford and in the North East. Newcastle, Sunderland and Middlesborough had placed the dock at his disposal but other than that it had all been Lessford. False Pretences, Credit by Fraud and Falsification of Documents had been his forte.

Nor had his 'arresting officers' ranged as widely as his pal. One detective inspector and, every other time, a detective sergeant. At Lessford Dooley and Wilkins had felt his collar, as had Detective Sergeant Stevens.

He'd been married, the father of three kids, but separated from his wife.

One strangulation. Location: Carmile Crescent. Name of victim: Anthea Carter, also known as Ann Cooke, also known as 'Queenie'.

Lessford, born and bred. Very much the enthusiastic slag. Other than a conviction at Blackpool for Conduct Likely to Cause a Breach of the Peace (which could mean just about anything) all other convictions were at Lessford and all had to do with indecency or prostitution. I knew the 'Anthea Carters' of this world. Every copper knows

39

them and counts them as a thundering annoyance. They hawk their wares too openly and cause a nuisance, instead of having a little discretion and keeping their legs crossed in public.

The arrests had all been made by uniformed officers. Usually policewomen. With the exception of one arrest by Detective Sergeant Wilkins.

I stacked the three files neatly at one corner of the desk. It was something with which to keep my hands occupied after this first quick run-through. The tenuous links were there, of course. Calladine must have seen them. Whatever else, he'd been a detective superintendent, which meant that, whatever else, he hadn't been the complete mug.

What (for example) are little snouts made of? For sure, civic-mindedness doesn't come into it too often. The guy who bawls and shouts his criticism of the police rarely has anything to offer other than empty opinions. Snouts, in the main, are hooks who grass on their mates. They curry favour with coppers, in the hope that their own misdeeds might be overlooked. They don't *like* coppers. They try to *use* coppers . . . but, if the copper knows how to peel his own onions, *he* uses *them*.

Therefore?

Using Detective Sergeant Wilkins as one thread which stitched the three killings together, what might be some sort of educated guess? That being Wilkins's informant was a slightly lethal occupation?

It seemed possible. It was an avenue worth exploring. I certainly needed to have a tête-à-tête with Detective Sergeant Wilkins in the not too distant future.

But – one step further – that didn't make Wilkins the bad apple. It might make him slap-happy in the manner in which he met and received griff from his informants, but the information was going the right way. Assuming the educated guess was on the button, the information was travelling from 'them' to 'us', which was as it should

40

be. My brief was to dig out how information was travelling from 'us' to 'them'.

Again, maybe Wilkins could help.

There was also the 'Carmile connection'. Keanan had been knifed in Carmile Street. Carter had been strangled in Carmile Crescent. The two couldn't be very far apart. Cities are built that way.

I made a mental note to buy myself a good street map as soon as possible.

11

Sugden was almost human.

I was deliberately about ten minutes late. I could, just as easily, have been ten minutes early, but if anybody was going to be left waiting and uncertain it was going to be Sugden. It hinted that he was not quite as important – quite as awe-inspiring – as he thought he was. Sure, he had the rank, but he didn't *own* me.

The ploy worked . . . more or less.

'A busy first morning?' he asked.

'Grant's been showing me around headquarters building,' I lied.

'I doubt if *he* knows his way round.'

'Main CID office. Communications Room. The way to the nearest toilet. That sort of thing.'

'How's the head?' Then, before I could answer and as a waitress approached the table. 'Try baked potatoes with cottage cheese and celery.'

I took his advice, ordered, and we settled down to eat.

Midway through the meal I said, 'Calladine?'

'What about him?'

'What was he like?'

'An odd thing to ask.' He frowned as he lifted a loaded fork to his mouth.

'Follow in somebody's footsteps,' I said. 'It helps to know how long his strides were.'

'Moderate strides.' He chewed as he spoke. 'He was no giant, if that's worrying you.'

'Comforting.' I bit into a stalk of celery. I added, 'Three undetected murders – three in a row – tends to chop even a giant down to size.'

'The streets are a little cleaner for their passing,' he grunted.

'Is that why they weren't detected?' I teased.

'That's the one you're allowed today,' he growled warningly.

'Eh?'

'The snide observations. Don't make it a habit, Lyle. Be warned. I dislike smart-arse coppers – whatever their rank.'

'But, three in a row.' I politely pressed my luck. 'I'm told they were gang killings.'

'Who told you that? Gilliant?' The double question was a very swift rebound to my remark. Maybe a little too swift.

'You may not believe this,' I smiled, 'but even Rogate has *some* criminals. They talk. Sometimes what they say is heard. The bush telegraph spreads the news – especially bad news.' He still looked unconvinced, and I added, 'Gilliant's on holiday. Remember? Devon, somewhere, I'm told. I don't know the man. Like the murders, I only know what I've heard.'

'You seem to have remarkably keen ears,' he rumbled.

'Nevertheless . . .' I lifted a quizzical eyebrow. 'Gang killings?'

'It's possible,' he admitted, but it was a grudging admission.

42

We fed ourselves in silence for a while. It was simple, wholesome food, which was more than could be said of the atmosphere I'd deliberately built up between us.

Coppers like Sugden like to figure themselves as the fount of all knowledge. Most of the time they nudge themselves ahead of the field and become very miffed whenever they have the feeling that somebody else is running alongside them, neck and neck. It tends to prick their precious ego slightly. Because of their rank they are gold-plated but, for much of their life, they work at conning the world they are twenty-four carat.

Sugden was *not* twenty-four carat . . . quite.

I allowed him time enough to live with the realisation before I probed a little deeper.

'A creep called Adams,' I said, quietly. 'Foster Adams. Known to his enemies as "Sweet F.A.".'

He chewed what was in his mouth, swallowed and sipped tea before he answered.

'Foster Adams. A very upright citizen,' he said eventually.

'That's not what *I'm* told.'

'Check with CRO. Check our own Criminal Records Department.'

'And every soldier's a hero,' I mocked. 'And every goose a swan.'

'Nor do *I* believe in fairies,' he agreed. 'But whilever he's firmly fixed to the top of the Christmas tree, what else?'

'Chop the whole bloody tree down,' I suggested.

'And if the axe slips? If the chain-saw goes out of control?'

'Set fire to the whole damn forest.'

'You're a dangerous man, Lyle.' He spoke slowly, then nodded as if in confirmation of his opinion. 'I think you would, too . . . if necessary.'

'Bet on it,' I assured him. 'Adams's tenure of his personal Eden has a very limited period to run.'

12

Red-necked police talk comes easily and that, too, I knew. I hadn't been out to impress Sugden. Sugden himself was of the old-fashioned, hard school. In the force – in every force – his was a dying and already rare species.

But (hopefully) because he might think he'd met somebody of a like kind, he'd talk. He'd recount our conversation – or at least the gist of it – and eventually (and, again, hopefully) news of the talk would reach the guy it had been aimed at.

And that guy – whoever he was – would report the conversation to Adams.

The object of the exercise was to cause ripples. To get movement, and as much movement as possible, because without movement nobody – and especially not Adams – was going to trip and break his damn-fool neck.

Meanwhile, I spent the rest of the afternoon getting to know people. In particular, getting to know Detective Sergeant Frank Wilkins.

He was in the basement of the headquarters building, at the indoor range. He was, I learned, part of the Emergency Assault Group and that, of itself, made him a little special.

I stood to one side, slightly out of his line of vision, and watched him blast off with a standard issue S and W .38. He held the revolver firmly but easily in a two-handed grip. His stance was the approved flat-footed half-crouch. As the life-sized, cardboard-cut-out targets jerked into view he lined up the weapon and squeezed off two quick rounds. He never missed. Nor did he fire at the 'Joker' targets – the figures representing innocent people – which the range master flipped up occasionally in an attempt to faze the marksman and, at the same time, underline the fact that, in real life *O.K. Corral* tactics would not be tolerated.

I watched while he emptied then reloaded three times. I was impressed. I strolled over to the range master – a ramrod-backed uniformed sergeant whose chest ribbons included the Military Medal. I introduced myself, then glanced to where Wilkins was emptying more used cartridges on to the firing counter.

'Are they all like him?' I asked.

'They're all good.' The range master was obviously proud of his protégés. 'When we decided to form an EA group it was agreed that only the best would be included.'

'Is it used much?'

'What?'

'The Emergency Assault Group.'

'It varies.' He sucked his lips as he performed mental calculations. 'Maybe twice a year. Maybe only once. We were once called out three times in six months – but that was unusual. We're the last resort but when we're wanted we're wanted in a hurry.'

'No earmuffs,' I observed. 'Or is that just Wilkins's foible?'

'No earmuffs.' His disgust showed itself. 'Those are guns, not peashooters. You get used to holding 'em, you get used to aiming 'em, then get used to the kick-back, you get used to the noise. Otherwise you blink when you should be watching.'

'Hit the wrong people?'

'Aye. Or don't hit the *right* people.'

45

'I'm impressed,' I smiled.

'They tell me you're from Rogate-on-Sands, sir.' I think he slipped the 'sir' in because he wanted to change the subject to a more personal level. He added, 'That's what I'm told.'

'Rogate-on-Sands,' I agreed.

Wilkins was cleaning the revolver. He'd threaded a piece of four-by-two into the eye of a cleaning rod and was working a hint of gun-oil into the barrel.

'I once spent a holiday there,' mused the range master. 'Just me and the missus. First time we could leave the kids to fend for themselves.'

'It must have been an exciting experience,' I said sardonically.

'Not really.'

'No?'

'Very quiet . . . but that's what we wanted.'

'More wheelchairs per square inch than Eastbourne.'

'Bit of a change coming here, sir?' He made it into a question.

'Promotion, sergeant.' My smile was slightly lop-sided. It went with the coloured eye and the stitched forehead. I must have looked very piratical. I added, 'People do some bloody stupid things for promotion.'

Wilkins had finished cleaning the Smith and Wesson, had opened the doors of a wall rack and was threading a thin chain through the trigger-guard of the revolver.

'No holster?' I murmured.

My voice startled him, he turned, saw me for the first time and began, 'Who the devil are—'

'Lyle,' I interrupted. 'Detective superintendent. I took over Calladine's office, this morning.'

'Oh! I'm sorry. I didn't know.'

'I didn't expect you to know, sergeant.' I glanced at the weapons in the gun rack and repeated my question. 'No holster?'

'It's my own gun, sir.'

'Oh?'

'We have a Force gun club. I'm a member. When we need to mobilise – as an Emergency Assault Group – most of us use our own guns and borrow holsters from the sergeant there.'

He padlocked the chain into position, closed the doors of the wall rack and glanced at my face.

'Had an accident, sir?'

'Of a sort.'

'It looks painful.'

'I could live without it.'

We walked alongside each other from the range and up the steps to the ground floor. It seemed necessary that I play 'first impressions' games. He was youngish – mid-to-late-thirties – and the spring in his step suggested he was physically fit. He could pop a .38 off without cringing and, from what I'd seen, he could usually hit what he was aiming at. His arrest record showed that he was prepared to close a cell door on the opposition whenever necessary. The way he talked hinted at a nice mix of deference and independence and the way he dressed – lightweight polo-necked sweater, corduroy trousers and Hush-Puppy-style shoes – showed that he recognised the appropriate gear suitable for a working jack ... not the near-obligatory unbelted mac, the single-toned tie and the battered note-book peeping from the side pocket of a tweed jacket.

The plus signs outnumbered the minus, therefore I took a chance.

I asked, 'What's your programme for the rest of the day?'

'Paperwork, mainly.'

'Urgent?'

'When *isn't* it urgent?' he grinned.

'Leave word at the desk,' I suggested. 'If you're wanted urgently, you're in my office.'

13

Holding a top-strap CID rank had its advantages. I'd sent one of the hewers of wood and carriers of water out to a local supermarket for a bottle of Haig and now Wilkins and I were sipping well-watered-down whisky while we relaxed and enjoyed a man-to-man parley. While I quietly pumped what information I could from a man I'd been lucky to find.

'I was born here,' he said. 'I know them all. Knew them, even before I became a cadet. Went to school with a few of them.'

'Foster Adams.' I held out an opened packet of cigarettes and as he took one said, 'The name's cropped up a couple of times. I gather he's quite a local character.'

'That's one way of putting it.' He struck a match and lighted my cigarette before he touched the flame to his own. As he waved out the match he continued, 'His father was a local bookie, before off-course betting became legal. Balsam Adams – the family seem to go in for fancy names. When the old man died Foster took over. Expanded. He started a local estate agency, then bought clapped-out property, converted it into bed-sits and did a "Rachman". Ducked from under before he could be prosecuted, sold his betting shops when off-course betting was legalised and branched out into cafés and nightclubs. Rumour has it that that's about the time he reached his first million.'

'Bent?' I asked.

'As your elbow,' he answered flatly.

'No previous convictions though . . . I've checked.'

'Never seen the inside of a court, sir. Except, maybe, as a spectator.' He drew deeply on the cigarette. His eyes hardened a little as he said, 'Three killings, by my reckoning. Oh, he didn't handle the knife – he didn't pull the strangling cord . . . but he *paid*.'

'Charles Barnes, Joseph Henry Keanan and Anthea Carter,' I murmured.

'I knew them all. I rather *liked* Joe Keanan.'

'You knew them all. You arrested them all,' I said pointedly.

He nodded, but didn't immediately rise to the bait.

'I'll ask a question, sergeant.' I paused long enough to lift my cigarette to my lips, then lower it. 'You can answer it, or you can tell me to go to hell . . . and no come-back.'

'They were all three my informants,' he said sombrely. 'And – because they *were* my informants – they were murdered. Is that what you're getting at, superintendent?'

'No man,' I said, 'could demand a straighter answer to a question he hasn't yet asked.'

In a voice which held very little tone, he continued, 'I even know the name of the murderer. Jean Baptiste . . . would you believe?'

'French?'

'From Marseilles. Imported as top frightener – executioner-in-chief – on Adams's payroll.' He leaned forward a little, then continued, 'If this conversation is being taped, I'm done for.'

'It's not being taped.'

'We're *both* done for . . . if it's being taped.' There was the barest hint of a tremor in his voice as he talked. 'You want to know about Adams, Superintendent Lyle? Okay . . . the simple facts. Prostitution. More than half – maybe as many as two-thirds – of the street women work for *him*. The brothels, the blue film clubs, the massage parlours, the strip joints. Those he doesn't own pay him a levy. Ditto the legitimate nightclubs. Check the payrolls of half the boozers, half the hotels, in Lessford.

49

There's always two or three – up to half a dozen – names of non-people. They don't exist. Mickey Mouse names . . . but they cover the tax Adams demands for comparative peace. He calls it "insurance". *We* call it "protection".

'How many coppers has he in his pocket? Your guess is as good as mine. He hasn't *me* . . . but that's the only one I'm sure of. I don't think he's had time enough to grab *you*. Yet. But he'll try. If he makes an approach, and before you tell him about this conversation, do me a favour. Give me twenty-four hours' start.'

He tipped booze down his throat and as the bottom of the glass was lowered on to the desk top it rattled very softly.

'You're scared,' I accused gently.

'Superintendent Lyle, I have sense enough to *be* scared.'

'Was Calladine scared?'

'Calladine was . . .' He moved his shoulders. 'Who the hell knows *what* Calladine was? He rarely moved from this office. He spun webs. In honesty, I think he tried his damnedest to snare Adams. I have the feeling he tried to fit him up a couple of times. He failed.'

'Because Adams was warned?'

'Why else?'

'Could he be fitted up?' I asked.

Again, the shrug.

'Damnation, sergeant!' I felt a wave of anger. I seemed to be losing this detective sergeant, and I *needed* him. The impression was that he knew more about this character Foster Adams than any other copper I'd yet met. I said, 'My first day in this office. I'm picking up three unsolved murders. You say you can name the killer . . .'

'Jean Baptiste.'

' . . . so what the devil makes the solving of those murders impossible?'

'There's a wall around him. There's a wall around the whole set-up.'

'A wall?'

'A wall of silence. A wall of fear.'

'For Christ's sake!'

'Look, sir.' He tapped the desk top gently with the empty glass, to emphasise his words. 'You say three murders. *I* say anything up to a dozen over the last few years. Not "reported" murders. Missings From Home. Some of 'em just . . . y'know . . . *died*. Some just disappeared. Believe me – *don't* believe me – it doesn't matter a damn either way.'

'As big as that?' Even I couldn't keep a tinge of awe from my voice.

'At least as big as that.'

'And you can say that with some degree of certainty?'

'With *absolute* certainty.' The grin was twisted and bitter. 'I'm alive, because I saved his daughter's life. The other three – Barnes, Keanan and Carter – were a warning . . . to *me*. Any nearer and *I* get the chop.'

'What does "near" mean?' I pressed.

'A few light years from an arrest, if that's what you're asking.'

'Nevertheless . . .' I drained my own glass, then said, 'Tell me about his daughter. Tell me how you saved her life.'

14

I ended my first day as a detective superintendent. I ended it in comfort and, maybe I was kidding myself, but I ended it with the feeling of some slight progress made.

I'd checked the current Egon Ronay and I'd booked in at the top-priced hotel in Lessford. The Eagle Arms. It was way beyond the depth of my purse, but that was okay. I took over a mini-suite – bedroom, bathroom and tiny lounge – booked it for a week and mentally crossed my fingers.

One week. That's what I gave myself. With Faber on the inside, plus what I'd forced from a reluctant Wilkins it seemed possible. Anyway – what the hell? I had a sympathetic bank manager back at Rogate-on-Sands.

I relaxed into a remarkably comfortable easy chair and congratulated myself on winkling out friend Wilkins.

Wilkins, as a man, was something of a mental mutation. As a copper he was one of those one-in-ten-thousand officers necessary when hell pops and blind anarchy is on the point of taking over. On the other side he would have been on a par with Jean Baptiste. In wartime he would have filled a niche reserved for undercover legends.

There was no compassion in his make-up. That was why he was in the Emergency Assault Group. He could squeeze the trigger of that .38, send somebody to kingdom come as casually as the average copper could give a verbal warning for speeding.

In the office I'd taken that hint of a shake in his voice as controlled emotion. Not so. It had been pent-up fury against Adams, because Adams had out-smarted him.

Adams had been on his way up when Wilkins, then a detective constable, had decided to nail him. Not because Wilkins had given too much of a damn about Adams's antics but because, being the cute rogue that Adams was, nobody had been able to nail a charge on his door. Wilkins had wanted to make DS. Adams inside a prison cell had seemed a short distance between two points.

The object had been to get close and one way of

getting close had seemed to be via Adams's daughter Caroline.

Caroline had been one of the great outdoors girls. Maybe she'd known about her old man's way of life but, if so, it hadn't worried her too much. Nor had it worried her friends (assuming *they'd* known) but that, too, had been not too unusual. Morals are elbowed aside if the wall of bank notes is high enough.

She'd been a member of Lessford Rock Climbing Club which, to further his own interests, Wilkins had joined, and for some time he had expended surplus energy clawing a way up various rock faces around the United Kingdom. He'd buttered up Caroline, they'd become buddies. So much so that there'd been an unofficial understanding that when she reached the ripe old age of twenty-one they'd be engaged.

Old man Adams?

Either he'd been dumb or too clever for his own good. The chances are he'd known Wilkins was a cop, but maybe he'd figured himself fireproof. On the other hand, maybe he'd worked out the possibilities supposing he had a son-in-law in the force.

Whatever . . . Kilnsey Crag had upset the applecart.

Kilnsey Crag is a very fancy piece of rock. It includes an overhang which necessitates the equivalent of crawling your way across a ceiling. And this at one hell of a height from the ground. It can be done, by those who like risking their damn-fool necks, as long as the pitons hold, but when Caroline Adams tried the journey, one of the pitons *didn't* hold.

In rock-climbing circles it was apparently headline news. Caroline bouncing around like a money-spider, at the end of a rope, and Wilkins up there with her, his hand jammed into a crevice, and the only thing between her and the law of gravity.

Wilkins had ended up with a badly mashed hand and a

few strained muscles. Caroline's spine had taken too much strain, and she wouldn't walk, much less rock-climb, again. Wilkins's hand had mended but, not being of the stuff of which martyrs are made, he'd turned his back on pushing a wheelchair-bound wife around.

Instead, and still being anxious to nail Adams's hide to the nearest door, Wilkins had fallen back on the old-fashioned snout-milking. End of Charles Barnes. End of Joseph Henry Keanan. End of Anthea Carter. And, any more hanky-panky business, end of Detective Sergeant Frank Wilkins.

But, at least he'd made DS.

There wasn't enough meat in it to make a movie but at least it gave me some small idea of the underground comings and goings in the fair city of Lessford.

15

It was a heftier breakfast than I normally eat but, the hell, I was paying for it, so I worked my way through eggs, bacon, sausage, kidneys, mushrooms and fried bread, followed by toast, marmalade and coffee. I could, I decided, skip lunch and tame the calorie count that way.

I smoked a post-breakfast cigarette as the waitress cleared the last of the wreckage from the table. I took a chance and put a few questions.

'You from Lessford?' I asked.

'Oh yes, sir.' She didn't mind talking. She knew it wasn't a pick-up. She was old enough for the wedding band to be biting into the flesh of her finger and, for sure, I was no Lochinvar.

'You know the town?' I pressed.

'I should. I've lived here all my life.'

'Carmile Street. Carmile Crescent. D'you know where they are?'

'Hallsworth Hill way, sir.'

'What sort of a district?'

'Y'know . . .' She see-sawed a hand, expressively. 'It used to be better than it is now. It's been going downhill for a few years.'

'Slum?'

'Oh no, sir.' She looked almost shocked. 'Not *that*. Just that . . . y'know . . . used to be accountants and the like. Now most of it's factory workers, clerical staff. That sort of thing.'

I wondered where the hell middle-aged waitresses fitted into her personal classification of occupations but later that morning, when I visited Hallsworth Hill district, I knew what she meant.

It had once been a classy area. It was now classy with crappy edges. The grass verges were litter strewn. The hedges were untrimmed. Graffiti had been scrawled on bus shelters and telephone kiosks. The houses were good and well built, but too many of them were in need of a lick of paint and, here and there, like a fungus eating its way to the surface, minor vandalism was taking over.

'It used to be a good district, sir.'

'So I'm told.'

I'd contacted the local beat bobby and we were strolling the pavements, side by side. He had a beer gut, and nose to match, but he seemed to know his patch and was ready to talk.

We turned into Carmile Street and he flipped a hand towards a house opposite.

'That's where they lived,' he said.

'"They"?'

'Keanan and his fancy piece.'

55

'Had he one?' I was interested.

'Oh, aye. When he'd been murdered she moved out, of course. Not far, though. Only round the corner to Carmile Crescent.'

'To—'

'Then somebody strangled *her*.' He shook his head, slowly. 'Bloody funny, that. Two of 'em, and they both get done in.'

'Let me get this straight.' I stopped almost opposite the house he'd indicated. We faced each other. I suspect my own expression was one of outrage. His was one of puzzled surprise. I snapped, 'Keanan and the Carter woman were living tally before he was knifed – right?'

'Common-law wife, sir.'

'I don't give a damn what sort of fancy name you give it. They were living *together*?'

'Yes, sir.'

'Then why the hell didn't you *tell* somebody?'

'They – they knew, sir. They—'

'"They"?'

'The – the – y'know ... the men on the murder inquiry.'

'*You* were on the bloody murder—'

'Oh, no, sir.' He shook his head ponderously. 'I wasn't on the inquiry team, sir. I had beat duty to perform.'

'Are you telling *me*—' I choked, then grabbed my flying temper and spoke more slowly and with a little less fury. After all, it obviously wasn't *this* slob's fault. I said, 'A man who lives on your beat is knifed to death, and *you* aren't brought in to provide what background detail you can?'

'I wasn't asked, sir.'

'Dammit, he was *killed* on your beat.'

'Yes, sir. Within yards of where he lived.'

'*She* was killed on your beat.'

'That's right, sir. Again, not far from where she'd gone to live.'

'And – again – you're not even consulted? You're not even *asked*?'

'No, sir.'

'Jesus, how crazy . . .' I took a couple of deep breaths, then snarled, 'Constable, I've seen those murder files. I spent most of yesterday morning reading the blasted things. Not a mention! Not so much as a hint! Two separate people. Keanan and Carter. That's all. Nothing about them sharing the same house, much less the same bed. What the hellfire sort of a murder inquiry is *that* supposed to be?'

'Sir, I'm not responsible for—'

'You're responsible for this bloody beat, man. The beat and everything that happens on the beat.'

'The ordinary things, sir.'

'What the hell do you call "ordinary"? Dogs pissing up against lamp-posts?'

'No, sir. But not *murder*.'

It was an argument I couldn't win. I knew his kind. I'd met too many of his kind. The idea of appearing in any court above that in which a bench of magistrates officiate scares the living crap out of them. They stick to motoring offences, and as few of *them* as possible. Anything bigger and they pass the buck and, moreover, the system is such that they *can* pass the buck. There is always a DC ready and willing to pick up an easy collar.

This type of thick-headed wooden-top never gets promoted. He doesn't expect to be promoted. He doesn't *want* to be promoted. He never gets his earhole punched, because he always walks the other way. Always! Send him to a punch-up and he'll take as devious a route as possible and walk as slowly as possible; by the time he arrives the blood is already congealing and the ambulances have already shifted the injured from the scene.

With luck, every witness will have disappeared into the far distance.

He knows every trick in the book when it comes to ducking from under. He is blind, deaf, dumb and stupid whenever any sort of decision is expected to be made. And – dammit! – every force in the land has its share of such men.

Nor can they be kicked out of the force. They never do anything wrong. They never do anything wrong, because they never do *anything*.

Therefore, I couldn't win. But, sure as hell, I could make the fat-gutted dumb-bell sweat.

I took him round a corner, out of earshot of any innocent little ratepayer and, for all of twenty minutes, I lashed every plain and fancy question I could come up with into his face. I had the sweat running down his fat, stupid chops in rivers.

How long had he known Keanan?

Since he'd taken over the beat about ten years ago.

How *well* had he known Keanan?

Enough to say 'Hello' or 'Good evening'. No more than that.

What about Keanan's previous convictions?

He didn't know Keanan *had* previous convictions.

What had Keanan done for a living?

He didn't know. He'd never asked.

I asked those sort of questions, plus a score of spin-off questions, and it was like throwing a tennis ball at a wet sheet. There was no rebound and I couldn't get through. He didn't even know Keanan had had a wife and kids.

I switched the questioning to the woman Carter. The result was pretty much the same. He knew they weren't married – but that seemed to be the general rule these days – and it hadn't seemed to be any of his business.

'Have you ever made *anything* your "business"?' I snarled.

'Sir, a man's private life is his private life. That's how I see things.'

Nevertheless, I threw questions at him. Questions I knew damn well he couldn't answer, and all the time I knew it was all a waste of time. One day he'd hand in his uniform and draw a pension and if he never answered a question between now and then he'd retire convinced he'd been a good copper. He hadn't made waves. He hadn't caused aggro. He'd kept his boots and his buttons polished . . . and that, by *his* yardstick, was the sum total of what he was being paid for.

And yet . . .

Somewhere, he *thought* there was a sister. He didn't know her name or where she lived. He wasn't one hundred per cent sure there *was*, but he thought so.

I gave him a final blasting, then left him to find a shoulder upon which to cry. Maybe I'd been rough with him. Maybe I was something of a bastard. Maybe my new rank had gone to my head.

Maybe a whole raft of things.

I walked away and didn't give much of a damn. Gilliant had upped my rank and asked me to do a job for him. This was only my second day and already I was making some small progress.

16

Let me tell you about the 'Mr Bigs' of this world; the would-be Mafia-type bosses who figure themselves as Godfather figures in the UK world of provincial crime. They are in a perpetual state of panic. They know the machinery of criminal law will – *must* – eventually catch them in its cogs and grind them into a soggy mess before dumping them behind high, granite walls.

Only give it time.   _U.S.A._

In the Land of the Free racketeering has been honed to a fine art. Even presidents have been known to accept rake-offs. A truly honest judge is something of an oddity and just about every cop has his price.

Not so in the English provinces.

Maybe we're too dumb. Maybe we're too scared. On the other hand, maybe we're too honest.

Not all of us, of course. That would be asking too much, and in every basket of eggs there is at least one which, if broken, stinks. But too *many* of us.

Which is why, and unlike their Yankee counterparts, the creeps of whom I speak do not live in high luxury . . . or at least not for long. They do not operate from penthouse suites. They do not sleep soundly behind bullet-proof doors. They do not have an army of trigger-happy 'soldiers' always there to pop holes in any inconvenient opposition.

In short, they *play* at gangsters, but without the true gangster's yearning for everlasting limelight, and when somebody craps on their personal doorstep, they worry. They almost bust a gut in their hurry to play Pilate and wash their hands of all guilt.

I was not, therefore, bowled over with surprise when I arrived back in my office and found a hand-delivered billet-doux sitting in the centre of the blotting pad. The expensive envelope had the words PRIVATE AND CONFIDENTIAL typed in the top left-hand corner. It was addressed to Detective Superintendent Lyle, Esq. The 'e' and the 'E' were both a little out of alignment.

Inside the envelope was a folded sheet of top-class paper. Blue-tinged with the motif of a boar in darker blue top centre. The typed message read:

60

Your company is requested at the
Blue Boar at 7.30 p.m. this evening.
A private dinner, in celebration of
your new position in our community.

There was a very elegant signature at the foot of the
message – 'Foster Adams'.

17

What with the breakfast at the Eagle Arms and the invitation to dinner at the Blue Boar I gave the Copper Saucepan a miss. I was, perhaps, ruining Sugden's day by not joining him for at least a coffee . . . but I would not have bet money on it.

Instead, I nosed around headquarters until I located the Force Records Office, then threw a little weight around until I obtained Calladine's personal file.

The sergeant clerk hummed and hawed a little. There was a certain amount of empty blather about 'confidentiality', but in the event rank counted.

Not that anybody would have paid a king's ransom for what information the file contained. It was couched in the usual crappy officialese and it told the tale of a very ordinary guy who, as a copper, had had a very ordinary career.

Name: James Edwin Calladine. Born: Halifax, 2 November 1933. Father: John Henry Calladine – Park Superintendent. Mother: Elizabeth Calladine – Housewife. Education: Primary school – no examinations passed. Pre-police occupation: counter assistant at local grocery store. Hobbies: football and stamp collecting.

In 1949 he'd joined the (then) Lessford City Police Force as a cadet. Two years later he was made full constable. In 1954 he received a Chief Constable's Commendation for 'perseverance while engaged on the detection of involved fraud' . . . but nobody had seen fit to be more specific regarding the type of fraud. A year later (at the age of twenty-two) he put his uniform in moth balls and worked as 'Aide-to-CID'. The next year (1956) he made it to detective constable.

In 1958 he married Margaret Hawkins, shop assistant. That same year he sat and passed his promotion examination; he passed it well enough to leap-frog the necessity of having to sit any future examination for inspectorship.

The next entry (1959) came as something of a surprise. He was ordained as a lay preacher in the Methodist Church.

1959 was quite a year for Detective Constable Calladine. In the October of that year his wife gave birth to his only child. A son, name Christopher George.

In 1960 he made detective sergeant and earned himself a second Chief Constable's Commendation but this time the generalities – let alone the specifics – weren't even recorded. Presumably for good, steady collar-feeling.

Nine years for detective sergeant wasn't bad going. Detective inspector in twelve years was even better. At that period of his life friend Calladine was motoring a little. Not a whizzer . . . but moving faster than most.

Then his progress skidded to something of a halt.

It took him seven years to bunk up to detective chief inspector, by which time he'd been a copper nineteen years. No more commendations. Just a normal, steady climb up the ladder.

The impression was that he was levelling out. He'd been a flyer, then something less of a flyer. The middle years merely showed a series of specialised courses he'd attended and the results of those courses hadn't been in any way spectacular. Then, in 1975, he'd upped himself to detective superintendent and the year after that the great 'amalgamation trick' had been pulled. Lessford City Police, Bordfield City Police and a great bite of the surrounding county constabulary had suddenly become Lessford Metropolitan Police District. Calladine had been given occupancy of an office at Lessford Headquarters, and that's where he'd remained until he'd argued the point with a hit-and-run motorist.

In 1981 he'd completed a thirty-year stretch. Thereafter – as his record showed – he'd attended a medical examination board each year to prove that he wasn't yet in his dotage. For eight years on the trot he'd blocked the promotion of five coppers of lesser rank.

Nothing unusual. Nothing outstanding. Nothing sinister. Open the personal files of eighty per cent of the senior coppers in the UK and you'd find a near-identical list of unimportant milestones in a life far removed from the fictional lawmen who detect multiple murder over their breakfast cornflakes.

Even the lay preacher bit. Lots of coppers – lots of ranking coppers – are part-time Holy Joes. Maybe some of them can dovetail the two jobs, but those *I've* ever met seem to go off the boil as practical thief-takers once they start getting the feel of the pulpit. Like Calladine. Maybe there's a reason. Maybe the 'humility' they preach doesn't sit too easily alongside the street knowledge needed to drag villains into the nearest nick.

How the hell can you dislike a dead man you've never even met? Nevertheless, that was *my* problem. Calladine had been a typical PC Plod with crowns on his shoulders. CID or uniform – there's not a hair's-breadth of difference. He'd been a yuck and (maybe because he *had* been a yuck) somebody had clobbered him in the small of the back with a motor vehicle.

I closed the file, sighed, and mentally decided to visit

Widow Calladine at the first opportunity. Maybe *she'd* seen something special in the creep.

18

You've seen one, you've seen them all. On a stage not much bigger than the average dining table a female with hard eyes and a rat-trap mouth was taking off her clothes to background music. Nobody was watching her eyes or her mouth. Not too many people were watching *her* . . . the clientele had seen it all before and this one was no Helen of Troy.

Other than the twin spots on the stripper, the lighting was blues and purples and deep reds. It hid the grubbiness and helped in the skilled miscount of change at the long bar at the rear of the room. There are a dozen such dumps in Soho. It would seem we had at least one in Lessford.

The frilly-pantied waitresses eased their way between tables too close for any degree of privacy and delivered food which, at an educated guess, had required a can-opener for the first stage of its preparation. The drinks were all in glasses with long stems and small holding capacity. The atmosphere was heavy with air freshener in a vain attempt to kill the background smell of stale perfume, old tobacco smoke and perspiration.

I almost wished I hadn't accepted the invite.

Earlier I'd returned to the Eagle Arms to clean up and change my shirt and tie. That, too, had been a mistake. The shower had sent its needle-spray on to my injured face and started a steady pump of pain which, until now, a couple of aspirins hadn't done much to relieve.

The dinner-jacketed bouncer had recognised me as

I walked through the door. He'd pointedly ignored my multi-coloured eye, given a jerky little half-bow from the waist and mouthed the welcome patter.

'Good evening, superintendent. Mr Adams is expecting you. If you'll come this way, please.'

Thereafter it had been all play-acting.

I'd pretended slightly more than mild interest in the slag publicly undressing herself. I tried for a gleam of partly hidden lasciviousness in my good eye. It wasn't easy. The truth was, I wouldn't have willingly accepted her as stand-in for my grandmother.

I followed the bouncer and we edged our way between tables at which sat the male and female mugs then, in a corner of the room, we slipped behind a heavy curtain, moved along a passage and round a corner and the bouncer opened a door and stood aside to let me enter Adams's private quarters.

I'd been ready for just about anything. I wasn't ready for what I got.

I'd lived long enough to recognise class and taste when I saw it. Not tinsel-covered flash. Not neo-lit gimmickry. The real thing, my friend. From the perfectly proportioned entrance hall, with a McCoy Persian rug the only covering to a polished floor any dance hall would have been proud of, with soft lighting illuminating buff-coloured walls on which were displayed a Diaz and a Delacroix which, at a guess, were neither prints nor copies, to the single piece of furniture – a brass-bound sea chest Morgan himself would have been proud to own – which stood alongside the door leading to the main rooms.

Nor could Adams's timing be faulted.

As the bouncer closed the door leading to the passage Adams himself opened the door leading from the entrance hall and advanced with a welcoming outstretched hand.

'Superintendent Lyle. It was good of you to come.'

If not scholarship, there was education in the voice.

65

A moderately deep voice, with a slight drawl. The hand-shake, too, was both firm and dry.

That was the moment when I decided Adams was going to be no push-over. There was the quiet arrogance of absolute certainty there. He knew – he *must* have known – that three killings were to be accounted for, and that responsibility for those killings was being eased, as much as possible, in his direction. I was a big wheel, albeit a new wheel, in the local law-enforcement set-up. My job was to put him where pigeons couldn't crap on him. Yet he treated me like a newly found acquaintance who might, one day, become a close friend.

So many surprises!

The immaculate cut of his charcoal-grey suit. The mane of near-white hair which gave clear evidence of a trim at least once a week. The ready smile which showed teeth white and even . . . *and* they were his own. The near-antique refectory table with six matching Hepplewhite chairs. The decoration matched the furnishing; the glass-ware, the dining service and the cutlery were, equally, part of a sense of elegance without flaw. As was the food. As was the wine.

And yet . . .

He seemed to read my mind and as he poured more wine into my half-empty glass he smiled.

'The punters,' he murmured. 'The strippers. The general atmosphere of the main room.'

'Not like this,' I agreed.

'They couldn't *afford* this.' He wasn't boasting. It was a simple statement of unarguable truth. 'Nor would they appreciate it. What we are drinking – enjoying, I hope – is Chablis Grand Cru Vaudesir. A fine wine, from a fine year. The people you passed on your way through the club would drink it like so much plonk.'

'But,' I teased, 'indirectly *they* pay for it.'

'Of course.' He moistened his lips with the wine before

66

continuing, 'I provide a service, Superintendent Lyle. I give a certain section of the public that for which they crave. It can be likened . . .' He moved an empty fork as he sought an appropriate analogy. 'It can be likened to cosmetic surgery. A face-lift. The removal of wrinkles around a woman's neck. Strictly speaking, not necessary . . . but pleasing to the recipient.'

'And, of course, cosmetic surgery doesn't come cheap.'

'*Very* expensive, superintendent,' he smiled.

The duckling in orange sauce, complete with all possible trimmings, was also expensive. Nor were we served by bare-legged hookers. Each course was wheeled in on a trolley and delivered to the table by two immaculately dressed waiters who knew their business down to the last spoon position.

Me?

I settled back, stopped being amazed, enjoyed the food and allowed the old railway car to roll along at whatever speed it wished. I was in no hurry. It was *I* who had accepted the invitation. It was *Adams* who had had the original idea.

We were in deep armchairs, sipping coffee and liqueur brandy and smoking green Havana cigars before we began touching the nitty gritty.

'Your face . . .' He tilted his head back, pursed his lips and sent a perfect smoke-ring spinning towards the ceiling. He murmured. 'I feel I should apologise.'

'You weren't the man who mugged me.' I smiled, then added, 'Were you? I didn't have time for a good look.'

'It happened opposite the Blue Boar.'

'One of your employees?' I asked innocently.

'No.' A second smoke-ring climbed towards the ceiling, then he straightened his neck, looked at me, and said, 'I have a reputation, Superintendent Lyle.'

'That much I've heard.'

'I run the top night spots . . . and other places.'

'Brothels?'

'I prefer to call them "places of pleasure".'

'And?'

'The gay community . . . they, too, have to be catered for.'

'Adams,' I warned, gently, 'you're talking to a senior police officer. Don't make *too* many admissions.'

'I provide a *service*.'

'I know . . . like cosmetic surgery.'

'Of necessity, the services I provide demand that I meet with – do business with – a certain class of person.'

'Bent?' I suggested.

'Not necessarily *bent*.'

'Slightly wavy?' I smiled.

'There are grey areas, superintendent.' The sigh was almost sad. As if it worried him to even contemplate fellow creatures being tempted into wrong doing.

'Grey,' I said, mildly, 'is the colour of dirt.'

'Do you . . .' He moved a slightly languid hand. 'Do you find anything "dirty" in your present surroundings?'

'Scrupulously clean,' I mocked.

'In that case?'

'What I don't see, I don't worry about. Is that it?'

'What you can't *alter*, you *accept*,' he corrected.

We smoked in silence for a few moments. Strangely, it was companionable silence. Maybe it was the meal, maybe it was the booze but, for whatever reason, I found myself rather *liking* the bastard.

Eventually he leaned a little farther back in his chair and said, '*You* have a reputation, superintendent.'

'Have I?'

'I've done my homework. You do things *your* way.'

'Don't we all?'

'But, more often than not, your way is a somewhat oblique way. Not by the book. Not the "official" way.'

'It has been known,' I agreed.

'I, too, have a reputation, Mr Lyle.'

'And I, too, have done my homework.'

He ignored the remark, and continued, 'I take it as a personal affront – one might say as an insult – when a man of your standing is robbed virtually on *my* doorstep.'

'Good of you,' I smiled.

'I do what I can to put things back on an even keel.'

I broadened my smile a little and raised my eyebrows. What the hell else? We were nearing the big trick of the evening.

He slipped a hand into the inside breast pocket of his jacket, then held the wallet out to me.

'Yours,' he said. 'Take it from me, there's nothing missing.'

'Fingerprints?' I suggested.

'*Except* fingerprints.'

'You know the thief?' I asked.

'An enterprising, but rather over-enthusiastic, gentleman.'

'*Very* over-enthusiastic.' I raised a hand to indicate my face. 'And his name?'

'He dropped the wallet.' Adams didn't even *try* to hide the fact that he was lying. 'It was found, and handed to me.'

'By one of the "grey" fraternity.'

'Exactly.' He chuckled, then added, 'I think more coffee and brandy is called for.' As he pushed himself from the armchair he said, 'I rather like you, Superintendent Lyle. In some ways, it's a pity you're a policeman. However, pomposity isn't part of your personality, and for such things we should be grateful.'

'A long and interesting conversation . . . is that what you're suggesting?'

'Why not? Unless, of course, you have more pressing matters to attend to.'

'Let's make a night of it,' I suggested. 'Let's *really* get to know each other.'

'Indeed . . . why not?'

It was past midnight when I left the Blue Boar. It was a new day – the first day of April – and I hoped that, of the two of us, I was the lesser fool.

19

'They have brawn, but very little brain.' Those were the words I'd used when selling Faber the idea of working from inside the Adams set-up. That's how clever *I'd* been. How wrong. How blinded by the stereotype picture of the clip-joint-owner-cum-boss-man-of-the-local-villains.

I was human enough – humane enough, if you like – to spend a few moments wondering what was happening to Faber. What might already have happened. Then I pushed the thoughts to one side. Faber was a hard man, and Faber had brains. That's why I'd picked him for the job. The chances were he'd still be upright.

I chewed my way through another man-sized breakfast and pondered upon the man I'd left in the early hours.

He'd talked a lot about 'reputations' – both his own and mine.

Reputations are not unlike heavyweight championships. They have to be fought for. They have to be earned. More than that, somebody has to be toppled from the top spot the hard way. Especially is this so in gangland. Somebody was there before Adams . . . obviously.

I sipped coffee, smoked the first cigarette of the day

and figured out possible ways and means of sneaking up on Adams via the back door.

20

Delaney. That's what the ancients of the CID Office had told me. Joseph 'Iron Man' Delaney, the king rat of the midden, before Adams had exposed the rust in his 'iron' and sent him scampering for cover.

'I've heard of him.'

Wilkins made the admission from the front passenger seat of the Cortina as we threaded our way through the canyons of high-rise outrages which made up much of North End. The area had once been the slum area of the city. It was *still* the slum area of the city. The only thing the combined efforts of architects and planners had done was to transform it from a horizontal slum into a perpendicular slum. The slobs had a larger area than before upon which to spray-paint dirty language and crudely drawn genitalian imagery. The stray dogs and cats had a few square yards of dying grass upon which to crap and urinate, supposing they could find space between the dumped and stained mattresses, the smashed prams without wheels and the general garbage which civilised people direct towards the local council rubbish dump.

'Not a lot.' Wilkins seemed eager to enter into some sort of conversation. 'The general run of Lessford crooks act as if to even mention the name Delaney might bring on an attack of the pox.'

'A handful in his time,' I assured him. 'Unlike Adams, he has form. GBH. Wounding. That class of offence. I'm told that, in his heyday, he crippled a couple of coppers . . . personally.'

'I'm going to enjoy meeting *this* bastard,' murmured Wilkins.

'Just give him time to talk, before you break his neck.'

'Oh, he'll talk,' promised Wilkins. 'He'll sing *La Traviata*, backwards, when *I've* finished with him.'

I didn't press the point. Coppers like Wilkins could be dangerous. At times, necessary – *very* necessary . . . but still dangerous.

We cruised through the streets in second gear and I noticed the groups of youths gathered at corners and under the porches which led to the entrances to the flats. I was reminded that a fair percentage of the population of Lessford were either coloured or half-caste. In my rummaging through the records of the criminal past of the city, earlier that morning, I'd come across the names of once-upon-a-time teenage gangs. The Goofballs. The Piccaninnies. That had been in Sullivan's time, when policing North End Division had entailed broken bones and blood on the tunic.

'You'd have liked Sullivan.' The place was getting under my skin a little. So much so that I'd voiced the opinion aloud.

'Who's Sullivan?'

'Superintendent – later chief superintendent – of this hell hole. Before they built the flats.'

'Tough?'

'Controlled aggression.' I kept my eyes skinned for the name Horbury Court. 'Before "neighbourhood policing" became the vogue. He played them at their own game . . . and won.'

'As it should be.'

'Sergeant Wilkins,' I warned, 'it may well be "as it should be" but it is *not* "as it is allowed" . . . at least, not officially.'

'More's the pity.'

'Just don't kill anybody,' I sighed.

72

I felt, rather than saw, his shoulder move in a silent chuckle. The truth was, I needed Wilkins. I was too old for street brawling and without much encouragement street brawling could be the end-product of any question-and-answer session in these parts. Indeed, I *needed* Wilkins . . . but wasn't pleased with the notion of *having* to need him.

I spotted the sign, Horbury Court, and braked to a halt. We were in the very arsehole of the city, we were strangers – at a guess, we'd already been earmarked as 'The Filth' – and I had the feeling of being watched by scores of suspicious eyes. The stench of the place even reached the streets. Every working copper knows all about that stench and until it has reached your own nostrils it can never be satisfactorily described. Dirt . . . but of course. Body dirt, old urine, unwashed clothes. All that and more. But with it there was also that foul and peculiar stench which comes from a combination of decay and disillusion – of hatred and hopelessness – of spitting contempt and a crazy desire to destroy.

This was, without doubt, the pits.

The group by the porch to the flats watched with narrowed, contemptuous eyes. Five of them. The leader had bleached, shoulder-length hair and wore a stained, brass-studded, leather waistcoat, skin-tight jeans and scuffed cowboy boots.

He was the boss-man by a mile, and he moved as if to bar our approach to the entrance.

Wilkins had swung himself from the car almost before the wheels had stopped turning. From a hip pocket he slipped a steel grip, and I knew we had at least one yob licked before any action got under way.

They were never in common usage and these days they are outlawed by every force in the land. Nevertheless, and quite unofficially, they *are* sometimes used. Coppers call them 'nippers'. They are a figure of eight made of tempered steel, with the smaller loop having a slight gap between the jaws so that they will encircle any size wrist. They are hinged to open, like sugar-tongs. The larger loop has a steel spring-clip which snaps into position once the smaller loop is in place around a wrist. From then on, all arguments cease. A sharp enough twist on the larger loop can break every bone in the wrist.

Wilkins reached 'Leather Waistcoat' and had the nippers on his right wrist before the yob had time to realise what was happening. Wilkins could handle nippers better than any other copper I'd met.

'Who the bleedin' 'ell—' It ended with a yelp of pain as Wilkins demonstrated what could be done.

'Who am I?' Wilkins turned the nippers and the yob's arm ended up behind his back with the fingers almost touching the shoulder blade. A second twist turned the yob until his face was touching the wall alongside the porch. In a gentle, almost conversational, tone Wilkins continued, 'I'll tell you who I am, Bozo. I'll tell you *exactly* who I am. I am the bearer of good news. If you behave yourself I *won't* snap your hand off at the wrist.' The yob's pals made a move as if to rescue their buddy. Wilkins continued, 'On the other hand – if you'll pardon the pun – any ballock-brained ideas on the part of *anybody*, and you'll have to grow used to the nickname of "Lefty" for the rest of your life.'

A twitch of the nippers had the yob almost screaming, 'Back off, you stupid sods. Back off! The bastard *means* it.'

I tended to agree, but remained an interested spectator.

With his free hand Wilkins was frisking the yob, and doing a very thorough job. A spring-bladed flick-knife and a cut-throat razor he dropped into one of the pockets of his jacket. The bowie knife he drew from the shoulder-sheath was too large. He tossed it in my direction and I picked it up from the pavement.

'We arrived in a car.' Wilkins's tone remained calm. His speech unhurried. He had a tiger by the tail and was surrounded by wild-cats, but seemed quietly unaware of any danger. He continued, 'When we leave, we leave by the same car. *You* will make sure of that, Bozo.'

He hoiked the by-now-whimpering yob to the Cortina, snapped adjustable ratchet-handcuffs on the left wrist then opened the door of the car and snapped the empty handcuff loop around the steel tubing of the front passenger-seat housing.

As he unclipped the nippers, he warned, 'This motor car. It is now in your care. Anything missing – if it's even scratched – when we come back and, for the first hundred yards, *you* stay hooked to where you are at the moment.'

We walked into the tower block and when we were climbing the stairs and out of earshot I said, 'Wilkins. Drop the anchor. I'd like to stay in this job a few years longer.'

'They don't know we're coppers,' he grinned. 'They don't know *me*. Sure as hell, they don't know *you*. The handcuffs aren't police issue. Nor is the wrist-breaker. We're like them. What *they* are. Hoodlums . . . but better dressed.'

21

In any self-respecting war, Wilkins would have won medals. He was damn near kill-crazy in his yen to topple Adams. And coppers shouldn't *be* like that. Hollywood coppers, perhaps – TV coppers – but not *real* coppers. He was distinctly kinky in the nastiest possible way. This,

I didn't give a toss about. But I figured I needed him – *and* his enthusiasm – if I was ever going to slap Adams behind the walls of one of HM prisons. I needed his madness. I needed his unique screw-'em-all attitude. But, if possible, at a point once removed.

I waited for Sugden to join me at the table in the Copper Saucepan and contemplated the events of that morning. The almost off-handed way Wilkins had tamed 'Leather Waistcoat' and his pals. The nippers and the ratchet-handcuffs. And the fact that Wilkins now had a bowie knife, a flick-blade and a cut-throat razor to add to whatever personal armoury he possessed.

Wilkins worried me a little. At a guess, Wilkins worried *everybody* . . . with the exception of Wilkins.

I had, in the past, thrown the book over the side. But never in the way I'd tossed it overboard that morning. And never with the cold-blooded enthusiasm which seemed to be Wilkins's way.

Sugden joined me and, after he'd complained about my absence the previous day, we ordered.

As we waited I said, 'Delaney. Joseph Delaney. Known, I'm told, as "Iron Man" Delaney.'

'A typical tearaway.' Sugden sniffed. 'One of the old fashioned boom-boom merchants. *And* a has-been.'

'I think he'd like to come again.'

'They'd *all* like to come again.' He was in a sour mood and did little to hide it. '*I'd* like to come again. Let me know what I know today, wipe twenty years off my life and make me a DS. Adams would be inside and they'd have melted down the key.'

'I think we should encourage him,' I said mildly.

'Eh?' Sugden glared.

'If he takes out Adams,' I said pointedly.

'Y'mean . . .' Sugden lowered his voice until it was a whispered growl. 'Lyle, are you seriously suggesting that we stoke up a gang war in Lessford.'

'If we help him chop Adams off at the knee-caps, we can bloody soon handle Delaney.'

'You've met him . . . have you? Delaney?'

'Adams *and* Delaney. Adams is super league. Delaney's second class. But, with *our* help—'

The waitress delivered the food and I stopped talking. But I continued to think and continued to remember.

Wilkins, working solo, could handle Delaney. He'd proved it. As Delaney had turned the knob to check who was hammering on the panels, Wilkins had lifted a leg, bent a knee and sent the door – and Delaney – shuddering back into the tiny hallway.

I hadn't needed to take my own hands out of my pockets. Wilkins had crossed the hall, yanked the middle-aged tearaway to his feet and thrown him into the grubby living room of the flat. He hadn't *quite* knocked him cold. But he *could* have, and *would* have . . . had it been necessary. It had been as neat a mix of martial arts and street brawling as I'd ever seen. And that, before anybody had said a word.

As he spooned sugar into his tea, Sugden said, 'We have three undetected murders on the books. Isn't that enough to keep you occupied for a while.'

'*You* have three undetected murders on the books,' I contradicted. 'I wasn't in this force at the time.'

'Good God, man! You can't—'

'Calladine couldn't detect them,' I reminded him. 'Word has it he was something of a whizz kid . . .'

'*I've* never said that.'

' . . . and, if *he* goofed – when he was on the scene within minutes – that means, as far as I'm concerned, that they *stay undetected* . . . unless, of course, *you* can produce rabbits from a hat.'

'You're paid a salary to do *something*, Lyle.'

I nodded, then sipped at my own tea.

'What exactly? In *your* opinion.'

'Shift Adams,' I said, bluntly.

'And substitute Delaney?'

'*Then* shift Delaney.'

We started our meal. The expression on Sugden's face suggested that what he was swallowing was causing mild indigestion. I didn't give much of a damn. The exchange had verified one very important point; that even Sugden didn't know my *real* job. That of rooting out the worm in the apple; of nailing the bastard who was feeding information to the opposition. Gilliant had kept *that* card very close to his chest.

I therefore chewed away happily, and congratulated myself on having had the good fortune to stumble across friend Wilkins. That boy could chew pig-iron and spit rust. He was my ace-in-the-hole . . . as long as I could control him.

The Beretta had shaken me a little. Why, God knows. A creep like Delaney had to have had a shooter somewhere in the house and Beretta Modello 1934s are as plentiful as snowflakes in an Arctic blizzard. The 'James Bond' gun . . . until somebody with more know-how than Fleming had pointed out that it *wasn't* the best handgun in the world.

I'd taken it, with a blink but without a murmur, when Wilkins had tipped the contents of a sideboard drawer on to the worn carpet and stooped to lift the Beretta from the rest of the junk. He'd unloaded it, dropped the cartridges back among the other stuff that had been in the drawer and had tossed the gun to Delaney.

'You might need it,' he'd said. 'If you're going to blast Adams into outer space, you *will* need it.'

'Who the hell says I'm gonna . . .?'

'*I* say. *We* say. This place has had too much of Adams. We'll try you for a change.'

'Who the hell are . . . ?'

'It matters not *who* we are. It matters not *what* we

are. Only what we've decided is of any concern to you, Bozo. And in our infinite wisdom we've decided that the Christmas tree needs a new fairy. You, instead of Adams. Or, if not you – if you haven't the bottle, if you can't find the muscle – somebody else.'

'You're coppers, aren't you?' Delaney's eyes had narrowed into slits of hate-filled suspicion.

'Off duty,' Wilkins had lied. 'Unofficial. We aren't even *here* . . . and we can prove it.' Then, in a whiplash tone, 'We're not in love with you, Delaney. Don't get any stupid ideas. You're an evil sod. But we're realists. We can't shift *every* evil sod from the face of the earth. Some we have to live with. We prefer living with you rather than living with Adams.'

'Coppers!' Delaney's whispered exclamation had carried near-disbelief.

'We aren't even *here* . . . remember? All we are are two shadows, offering you top spot on the shit-heap. Take it, or leave it.'

Sugden swallowed, emptied his mouth, sipped his tea then said, 'You say you've met Adams?'

'I had dinner with him last night.'

'Did you, by God!'

'At the Blue Boar.'

'At *his* place!'

I nodded.

Sugden lowered his knife and fork. He placed them, with exaggerated care, along his plate. He stared at me for about ten heartbeats before he spoke and when he *did* speak it was apparent that each word was chosen carefully and with great deliberation.

'Lyle, I give you credit for not being a fool.'

'Thank you.'

'You wouldn't have reached the rank – not even the rank of detective chief inspector – not even in a force like Rogate-on-Sands – without above average mentality.'

'I've known some dopey chief inspectors,' I smiled.

'I don't think you count yourself in their number.'

'Does anybody? Do *they*?'

'You're very devious, Lyle.'

'It's a complaint I've heard before.'

'I'm not *complaining*. I'm stating what is already the obvious. You're devious. You're not a fool. You might even be cleverer than I thought you were a couple of days ago.'

'You didn't know me then. You don't know me *yet*.'

'I know you had dinner, last night, with Foster Adams. *And* at the Blue Boar.'

'In his private suite.'

'And?'

'It was an excellent meal. He's a man of taste.'

'Hitler liked Wagner. *I* like Wagner. That doesn't mean I like *Hitler*.'

'I never met him.'

'Who?'

'Hitler. He died in his bunker when I was in my teens.'

'Don't smart-arse me, Lyle!'

I'd been baiting him and, for a moment, his anger surfaced. Then in a quieter tone he added, 'I'm serious, man. You need one hell of a long spoon before you start supping with a man like Adams.'

'Know thine enemy,' I quoted. Without ribbing him I added, 'This man – this Foster Adams – I have the feeling he's almost a cult figure. He holds this opinion. That he's un-get-at-able. More than that, he's sold this "beyond the law" gag to too many people ... including policemen. I wanted to meet him. I wanted to meet him on his *own* terms, and where *he* counted himself absolutely untouchable. In effect, he invited me into his parlour ... and I accepted the invitation.'

'Did he offer you?' asked Sugden.

80

'He offered me nothing . . . other than hospitality.'

'He will.'

Having delivered himself of this final and absolute truth, Sugden raised his knife and fork and continued eating as we talked.

'You say Adams *and* Delaney.'

'Delaney this morning.'

'You tend to get around a bit.'

'Delaney didn't invite me. I just arrived.'

'And?'

'He lives in a dump. He has a reputation as a wild man . . . which I very much doubt he deserves. He hates Adams. He'd like to take over Adams's spot, and I wish he would. With Delaney we could tie a string around his waist and use him as a yo-yo.'

I kept quiet about Wilkins. Sugden was, after all, an assistant chief constable and there are certain things assistant chief constables should *never* know. Even those cast in the Sugden mould.

Like starting a Cortina with a yelling yob still attached to the front passenger-seat housing. Like a detective sergeant grinning down at a terrified face as he unlocked the handcuffs from the yob's wrist. Like that same detective sergeant planting the sole of a shoe against the yob's shoulder and sending him skidding and sprawling as he slammed the car door and I moved from first to second.

The truth was, Wilkins terrified me – what Wilkins was capable of doing terrified me – but for the moment I needed him and I wasn't taking the risk of Sugden saying I couldn't *have* him.

'Delaney was a handful, once upon a time.' He forked the last of his meal into his mouth, chewed and swallowed then dabbed his lips with his napkin. 'He was almost as big a bastard as Adams, but less subtle. Given the chance, he just *might* be a handful again.'

'Mr Sugden,' I smiled, 'are you trying to frighten me?'

'A word to the wise. No more.' He finished what was left in his teacup and stood up to leave. He said, 'I'm getting your measure, superintendent. You don't frighten easily . . . if at all.'

22

It was closing to three o'clock and I'd already done the groundwork.

The guy to brain-pick if you seek the unvarnished truth about beat coppers is a good section sergeant. I'd typed Hamilton as that. He was boss man in the Radio Communications Room and he quietly hated the job and didn't pretend otherwise. He walked with a rolling limp and the limp was the result of an encounter with a bunch of rampaging North End yobs. Hamilton and one of the yobs had ended up in hospital beds. The accompanying constable and five other yobs had suffered the euphemistic 'cuts and bruises' before brass-buttoned reinforcements had arrived to mop up the gore. A smashed hip had taken Hamilton off foot patrol and dumped him in the RCR, from where he organised chases after stolen cars, triple-nine emergencies and road-traffic-accident attendances.

He was a good man wasted. He was the sort of man I sought.

'Somebody reliable. *Very* reliable,' I'd explained.

He'd nodded his understanding.

'Somebody who can recognise nawpings before they arrive . . . then clamp down on the bastard offering before he's even had time to put the offer into words.'

There'd been more slow nods, then he'd chewed his lower lip before muttering, 'I had a lad, sir.'

'A son?'

'Aye.'

'In this force?'

'Mellor Road Division.'

'Good policing stock,' I'd smiled.

'We like to think so. His uncle's in the Lancashire mob.'

'He'd take the job?' I'd pressed. 'Knowing what I have in mind?'

'He'd take the job, sir.' The certainty had been absolute. He'd added, '*And* he'd understand . . . if I have to draw him a bloody graph.'

From Hamilton I'd gone to Grant's office. Assistant Chief Constable (Admin.) Charles Grant. The man responsible for the hithering and thithering of the Lessford half of the force, including the disciplinary side of things.

I'd outlined what I'd wanted, but hadn't gone into specifics about my reasons for wanting it.

'Parker suspended,' I'd said.

'Oh, quite.' He'd frowned lofty agreement. 'Men like that – constables like that – they give the force a bad name.'

'A good man in his place. To tighten things up a bit.'

'I'll make—'

'I'm told there's a beat constable in the Mellor Road Division who's eager for a transfer to the City Division. He sounds to be the type we need.'

'Really? I always understood Mellor Road to be the place they *didn't* want to . . .'

'Constable Hamilton. Sergeant Hamilton's son.'

'Really? I hadn't heard young Hamilton was keen to be taken from . . .'

'That's what I'm told. It would solve our problems.'

'I suppose. I suppose.' He was an assistant chief constable. He wasn't too much of a mug. He'd frowned and remarked, 'You seem to have become very well acquainted with Lessford, superintendent. And in a remarkably short time.'

'Yes, sir.' I'd slipped in the 'sir' much as the peasant of a century ago touched his forelock. It meant damn-all, but it created a certain impression. 'It seemed a good idea. To get to know the place before I took over the superintendentship.'

'Oh, quite. Quite.'

It was like knitting gossamer. Very few assistant chief constables can be led by the nose. They know the power they wield and aren't shy of wielding it. On the other hand, they *can* be pointed in the right direction and given a slight nudge. That's what I'd done and, as I checked the photocopies of Parker's report and the Misconduct Form based upon that report, I figured that the pink ribbon was already in place and one more useless copper was ready for urgent delivery.

I wandered back to Grant's office and settled into a chair alongside him, behind the desk. I was there as a witness – if needed – but I had other reasons for wishing to be in at the kill. The secretary was in place, sitting quietly in the far corner of the office, pencil poised above the open notebook on her knee and ready to reduce whatever was said to the loops, dots and dashes of shorthand.

'Are we ready?' asked Grant 'and, when I nodded, he thumbed the bell-push on the desk top.

There was a moment of expectant silence before the force drill sergeant performed his party piece.

The office door burst open as a prelude to the bawling.

'Accused officer, quick march! Left-right-left-right-left-right. Mark time. Halt! Right turn. Stand to attention, man. Look your height. Eyes front, and speak when you're spoken to.' Then to Grant, 'Police Constable Frederick William Parker, *sir*.'

On the evening of the previous Sunday I'd promised Parker he'd be sorry. One Lessford copper now knew I kept my promises. His face was a mask of frozen panic as Grant read out the charge of Neglect of Duty.

'Do you plead "Guilty" or "Not Guilty"?' Grant asked the obligatory question.

'Guilty, sir.'

He hadn't much of a choice after what I'd made him write in his notebook. Grant emphasised the point.

'There are certain remarks in your report, Parker. Remarks which, I understand, Superintendent Lyle insisted you include in the report.'

'Yes, sir.'

'He ordered their inclusion.'

'Yes, sir.'

'Do they represent the truth?'

'Er – yes, sir.'

'Were they included under duress?'

'He ordered me to include them, sir.'

'Do they deviate in any way from the absolute truth?'

'No, sir.'

Grant gave a deep and slightly hammy sigh, turned his head and said, 'Mr Lyle. Have you any questions you'd like to ask this officer?'

Parker lowered his gaze to my still-discoloured face and, for a moment, the loathing pushed aside the panic.

The drill sergeant bawled, 'Look your height, man!' but, within that single heartbeat of time, Parker and I knew exactly where each of us stood. He was due to be nailed to the nearest door, and I was already swinging the hammer.

'A few questions about Adams.' I kept my voice quiet and controlled, but with enough grit and gristle in the tone to leave Parker in no doubt that the next few minutes would stay with him for the rest of his miserable life. 'A few questions about how much he was paying you.'

'I don't know what you're talking about.'

'Sir,' I reminded him.

'Sir.'

'I'm talking about keeping the area around the Blue Boar nice and quiet, Constable Parker.' I kept my tone gentle and steady, but it was the steadiness of a laser beam. This man was my fish, and I wanted him hooked, gaffed and filleted before he left the office. 'I'm talking about a man being mugged. Knocked unconscious and robbed. Never mind that that man was *me* – you didn't know that at the time. You were doing what Adams pays you to do. You were keeping his doorstep peaceful and free from police attention.'

'My job is to keep the peace, sir.' He made a puny fight of it. 'That's – that's what I'm paid for.'

'*Not* aggravated robbery?' I sneered gently. 'That's *not* what you're paid for? Whose "peace" are you talking about, Parker? Adams's "peace"?' I leaned forward slightly and put a little more snap into my words. 'Parker, you're on a Misconduct Form for Neglect of Duty. You've already pleaded "Guilty". You're not treading water, Parker . . . you're treading *air*. This thing – this business of paying officers backhanders for a continued quiet life – I'm going to nose around. I'm going to nose around a lot. Until I get to the bottom of it.' I paused, then said, 'At the moment, you're hanging on to that uniform by the skin of your teeth. Any more lying – any more no-sir-not-me-sir antics – and, unless I'm very much mistaken, you'll whistle goodbye to both it and your pension. I'll ask you once more. Be wise. Don't make me *prove* you're a liar. How much has Adams been paying you?'

He moistened his lips, then choked, 'Not money. I never took money.'

86

'Sir?' I teased.

'Sir,' he groaned.

'But?'

'I – I – we sometimes had a meal there.'

'We?'

'Me and the wife.'

'On the house, of course?'

'Y-yes, sir.'

'Complete with floor show?'

He nodded stiffly.

'Complete with floor show?' I rapped.

'Yes, sir,' he breathed.

'Slags stripping off in public. Soft porn. Sometimes something a bit more daring than *soft* porn. That sort of thing?'

'Y-yes, sir.' Now, it was little more than a whispered moan.

'Free food. Free booze. As much titillation as the house could offer. And, that's *not* bribery?' I mocked.

'In a – in a way . . . I suppose.'

'Sir?'

'Sir.'

'And, how often was this feast for the eyes and the stomach pushed in your direction, Parker?'

'About – about once a week, sir. Sometimes twice a week . . . but not twice every week.'

'And for what?'

'He – wanted . . . He wanted . . .'

'We can guess what he wanted, Parker. We can guess *exactly* what he wanted.'

'I wasn't alone,' Parker blurted.

'Of course not. You're not on duty twenty-four hours a day, and Adams wanted twenty-four-hour immunity from the inconvenience of police annoyance. Of *course* you weren't alone.'

'How many others?' Grant asked the question, and

this time the heaviness of his tone was not a put-on. This time the sigh was very genuine.

23

The Tops were all they'd been cracked up to be. And more. I'd known lonelier places in the wilds of Scotland and, no doubt, parts of the moon could make this place seem like Piccadilly Circus but, for me, this was one of the loneliest places on earth.

Yet some very plain and fancy crime had been committed on the Tops, and over the years this area had called for some equally plain and fancy policing. Near-legends had held the chief-superintendentship of this neck of the woods. Ripley, for example. Blayde, for example. And others. It had been part of the Beechwood Brook Division of the old county constabulary. It was still Beechwood Brook Division, but now it had been swallowed up in the impossible Lessford conglomerate.

I mused upon the tales told of these 'gods' of law enforcement as I steered the Cortina along the thread of tarmac which wound its way across an ocean of heather and fern. Here and there patches of bilberry or gorse broke the monotony but, other than that, the undulating moorland seemed to go on for ever.

I'd left Grant to sort out the Parker thing. There was corruption if not on a grand scale at least on a scale too widespread for the attention of a mere superintendent. Parker had named five constables and a uniformed sergeant who were also enjoying buckshee nosh, booze and entertainment at the Blue Boar. He'd been genuinely shocked.

Assistant chief constables, it seemed, could be remarkably innocent concerning what went on at street level.

His voice had trembled slightly as he'd said, 'You're on suspension till further notice, Parker.'

'Yes, sir.' And by his tone it was plain that Parker had realised that his crock of gold had been snatched from the end of his personal rainbow.

'Take him out, sergeant.' Grant had spoken to the drill pig. 'Relieve him of his warrant card, his staff and his handcuffs. And get the men named – wherever they are – here, to my office, immediately. They, too, are suspended from duty until further notice.'

'Yes, sir.'

Thereafter had come the left-right-left-right-left-right pantomime and when the door had closed Grant had asked the secretary to leave. To type out her notes and await his call.

When we were alone Grant had offered me a cigarette and I'd taken one. We'd talked as near man to man as our respective ranks allowed.

'You haven't been here a week, Lyle. You've already opened a can of worms. I should be grateful.'

'Not "grateful".' I trod warily. 'No chief is "grateful" when a newcomer stumbles across failings in the system.'

'Nevertheless . . .' He hadn't been able to find the right words, if only because the right words would have made *him* look a damn sight short of perfect. Instead, he'd tapped his cigarette gently against the rim of the glass ashtray.

We'd enjoyed a stretch of silence until he'd forced himself to remark upon the obvious.

'Six constables and a sergeant absent from the City Division. We need a quick reshuffle to fill the gap.'

'It's a big hole,' I'd agreed.

'It needs filling quickly. As soon as possible. There's too much valuable real estate in that division to do any paring down.'

'May I offer a suggestion, sir?'

'You made the hole.' The accompanying smile hadn't been one hundred per cent friendly.

'Sergeant Hamilton?' I'd suggested, gently.

'He's in the Communications Room. You've already—'

'The Communications Room can damn near run itself until a replacement is found.'

'He limps. He has a gammy leg.'

'He has a motor car. He's wise to every trick any skiving constable can come up with. A personal opinion, for what it's worth. We'll see the difference in the City Division within a month.'

'Fine.' He'd nodded, slowly. What we'd just uncovered had left him like a drowning man, gasping for breath and looking for a life raft. 'Hamilton as replacement section sergeant, but what about the shortfall on beat men?'

'Leave that to Hamilton.'

'What?'

'Sir – correct me if I'm wrong – but the chances are you haven't served in this force all your police career.'

'I don't see what the devil that has to—'

'It's the difference between you and Hamilton, sir.' I'd pressed on. Gilliant had given me the job and to do that job, I had to have certain types of men in certain places. The Grants of this world could go screw themselves . . . that is, if the job was going to get done. I'd added, 'It's important, sir.'

'I came here as assistant chief constable,' he'd admitted, tightly. 'In the same way you've come as a detective superintendent.'

'Hamilton's been in the force all his policing life.'

'Damnation, Lyle. I know this force. It's my *job* to know this force. It's a big force, but I claim to—'

'You didn't know about Parker. You didn't know about a sergeant and five other constables, all taking rake-offs from Adams.' I'd softened the clincher by adding, 'Sir . . .

how *could* you know? There are too many layers – too many filters – between them and this office.'

'And, Hamilton?'

'He's at ground level, sir. He's at grass roots. He either knows, or he knows people who'll *let* him know. The force needs him there, to straighten out the City Division. But give him a chance. Let him choose his own troops. With Adams he'll be up against some very heavy artillery. There'll be attempts at buying him off . . . if not in cash, in kind. Let him at least have the knowledge that the men *he* picks have the simple guts to tell Adams to take a flying leap.'

There'd been more of it, but that had been the point at which I'd known I was home and dry, with the bacon safely wrapped and ready for the grill. Grant hadn't had any valid arguments left. Parker and his free nights out at the Blue Boar had chopped him off at the knees. All Grant had been able to do was hum and haw a little, use fancy language in an attempt to switch the talk around until it had seemed to be *his* idea.

That was okay by me. Chief constables, assistant chief constables, that's part of their job – to pick brains and play at intellectuals!

24

I drove with the window of the Cortina wound down and with my right elbow resting on the sill. The car's slipstream and the wind, which seemed as much a part of the Tops as the heather and bracken, hit the side of my damaged face and created a continuous ache. I was, I decided, a masochist.

I was on my way to see Calladine's widow. To see whether he'd dropped any hints about how far he'd pushed the inquiry before his death. Some coppers work that way. Some make notes. Some store all the various facts in their brains and sometimes talk things over with their wives. Some make notes, but take the notes home with them; away from prying eyes and fellow coppers who might find them, jump in and grab the credit.

Policing is not a pure profession.

How the hell can it be? A good copper, by definition, is a good manhunter and manhunters, as a breed, take what's going and use it for their own ends.

I'd done it myself. I'd had it done *to* me.

But Calladine's widow just *might* have some snippet of information I could use.

I'd mentioned my plans to Hamilton when I'd called in at the Radio Communications Room to tell him about Grant's decision to move him to the City Division.

'And five new coppers,' I'd added.

'Which five?'

'Take your pick, sergeant. Men you know. Men you can trust.'

'From North End?' He'd sounded almost eager.

'Not *all* from North End,' I'd warned. 'Otherwise we exchange one shortage for another.'

'Trust me, sir.'

'I do . . . and God help you if you let me down.' Then, I'd added, 'Calladine. Where did he live? I think I should ask Mrs Calladine a few questions.'

'She won't be at home, sir.'

'No?'

'She's gone to live with Chris, her son, for a while.'

'Where does *he* live?'

'He farms a stretch Pinthead Pike way. Out across the Tops. Fairway Farm.'

He'd given directions and had ended, 'There's a fork in the road. You can't miss it. Take the right fork and about six miles along that road you'll find Fairway Farm on your right.'

The junction was coming up, with a lonely AA box sitting there waiting to welcome lost and miserable motorists. I eased the Cortina on to the right fork and allowed my mind to ask itself a few pertinent questions.

For example, Why *me*? And after that, What the hell was I trying to prove?

The three murders weren't my concern. If Wilkins was to be believed they'd already *been* detected. Some French bastard called Jean Baptiste had done the killing, and if Wilkins knew that Calladine *must* have known. But – agreed – detecting a crime and proving who'd committed that crime didn't always go hand in hand. Every street-wise copper knows of crime files gathering dust in the archives of a divisional office, or a headquarters office, and knows they'll keep gathering dust till Doom cracks. Not because the culprit isn't known, but because twelve goons sitting in a jury box would never convict after the combined hotshot cross examination and the hearts–and–flowers closing speech of an even moderately good defending lawyer.

So what the hell *was* I trying to do?

Repay Gilliant for handing me a superintendentship on a plate? Maybe that was part of it. I owed him *something*. At Rogate-on-Sands I'd just about hit the brick wall every copper faces when the top drawers are already filled. I was up a peg, I was drawing a bigger salary and, eventually, I'd draw a bigger pension . . . but that didn't answer all of the question.

Gilliant had pulled me in for a purpose. To sort out the apples, and to do the sorting as quietly as possible. To find the one –· maybe more than one – with the maggot in its flesh.

Fine . . . I'd already shifted seven badly bruised speci-
mens. But *the* one – the truly rotten fruit – had yet to be
found. It was there all right. I had that very important gut
feeling that it was *there*. Adams had been too sure of himself. The simple law of averages insisted that three killings
in a row couldn't be undetected – apparently *undetectable* –
without somebody in the know creating more blind alleys
than Hampton Court Maze.

Gilliant wanted the sly bastard taken out of circulation,
and he'd offered me the job. And I'd accepted. More than
that – and to this I could find no even part-reasonable
answer – I knew I wanted to hand boyo over to Gilliant
on the first day of his return from Devon.

Already I hated him . . . whoever he was. He'd made
the rest of the force look like a cageful of monkeys. He was
somewhere on those streets, somewhere in one of those
offices . . . *somewhere*. Having condoned triple murder he
was smiling a sweet smile while Adams patted his head in
gentle appreciation.

I suddenly found that my jaw muscles were becoming
a little cramped. I relaxed a little and kept a weather eye
open for a sign that read 'Fairway Farm'.

25

Margaret Calladine.

A snippet of near-forgotten memory. As a kid I had
a book of children's stories. One was called 'The Old
Lady Who Lived in a Vinegar Bottle'. Widow Calladine
brought the story back with a rush. Her hips were out-
rageously wide and her shoulders ridiculously narrow.
From the neck down that's exactly what she might have

been . . . a vinegar bottle. From the neck up she gave the impression of an ancient farmyard fowl who'd seen many a rooster knocked from his perch. Scraggy-necked, thin-mouthed and with a beak-like nose. Her hair clung to her skull like wire wool. It was anybody's guess what its true colour was. *She'd* decided it should be the colour of newly washed carrots. She had grey eyes – battleship grey with an everlasting glint of argument – and they rarely blinked.

Maybe she was still in mourning. It was hard to be sure. Her clothes were dark coloured and severe, but she was the sort of woman who *always* wore dark coloured and severe clothes.

She sat primly in an old-fashioned wooden rocking chair as she stonewalled the questions and left me in little doubt that my absence would be preferred to my presence. I didn't mind too much. I had a thick hide, and in the past I'd been given the refrigeration treatment by experts.

'It still hurts to talk about him,' she snapped . . . but she hid the hurt with apparent ease.

'I understand.' My mock sympathy matched *her* thespian accomplishment.

'Especially to *you*.'

'Really?'

'You're what he once was. *You've* taken his place.'

'The force needs a detective superintendent, Mrs Calladine.'

'Seeking me out shows a lack of feeling on your part.'

'I'm sorry you see it that way.'

'What else?'

'Bringing your husband's efforts to a successful conclusion?' I suggested.

'To me that's a poor excuse for bad manners.'

Her voice matched her outward appearance. Her vocal cords seemed to be made of spring steel and she bit off the words with the clean-cut finality of a guillotine.

'Adams?' I murmured tentatively.

'What about Adams?'

'Foster Adams?'

'I know who you mean. What about him?'

'He was your husband's enemy . . . right?'

'Of course. James was a fine policeman.'

'That I do not doubt.'

'He was a fine detective. A *great* detective.'

'They're very thin on the ground.'

'Adams was a criminal – still *is* a criminal – of course he was my husband's enemy.'

'You talked about Adams?'

'What?'

'Together. In private. When he was off duty. Man and wife talk. You discussed Adams?'

'James never brought his work home with him.' She rocked gently in the chair. She twiddled the thumbs of her linked hands in a steady, circular motion. She repeated, 'He *never* brought his work home. He knew how much I disliked dishonesty. How much I disliked criminals.'

Outside it was dusk and deepening into darkness. There in the kitchen of the farmhouse, the two sets of twin neon strips illuminated the room and gave it a clinical cleanliness.

It was a large room with a large, double-glazed picture window giving a view over farmland and, beyond, the rolling moorland of the Tops. The floor was of red tiles. The walls were of cream coloured tiles, ceiling high. The centrepiece was a massive, deal-topped table and the warmth – a steady, drowsy warmth – came from a three-hotplate Aga cooker which took pride of place along one of the walls. The lids of the hotplates were down, but the cooker pushed out enough warmth to more than counter the chill of the April evening.

'Every police officer dislikes criminals,' I smiled.

'Adams was a criminal. Still *is* a criminal.'

'You talked about him?'

'I've already told you. James didn't bring his—'

'Mrs Calladine, you must have *mentioned* him – your husband must have told you *something* about him – otherwise you wouldn't know he was a criminal.'

'He runs a club, some sort of nightclub, in the city centre.'

'The Blue Boar.'

'Is that what it's called?' She gave a single nod, then answered her own question. 'Yes. That's the name of the place. The Blue Boar.'

'Running a nightclub isn't a criminal offence,' I pointed out, gently.

'By *my* yardstick . . .'

'We're talking about your husband's yardstick, Mrs Calladine. As a police officer. As a detective superintendent. A mere nightclub owner wouldn't merit mention.' I paused, then added, 'Especially by a policeman who didn't bring his work home.'

'I find you objectionable, Superintendent Lyle.'

'I sometimes find *myself* objectionable, madam. Most men do . . . at times.'

'Adams . . .' She paused, then continued, 'Adams, too, was objectionable.'

'You've met him?'

'No. But James told me about his activities. He was a lewd man.'

'Lewd?' She was moving into deep water, and dragging me with her.

'He provided lewd entertainment.'

'Oh! I see.'

'Nudity. Fornication. Sinful things.'

'Art for art's sake,' I murmured. 'Beauty – and, presumably, ugliness – is in the eye of the beholder . . . so I'm told.'

'You're not a very godly man, superintendent.'

'Nor claim to be. Few policemen are.'

'James was.' The eyes glinted and took on a slightly different gleam. 'In his younger days. To hear him *preach*. To sit in the congregation and watch him, up there, voicing the word of the Lord. Giving comfort to the believers and a warning of everlasting damnation to those who denied the Almighty.'

It was a well-equipped kitchen. Purpose-built shelves housed full sets of gleaming copper pans. Good-class china was stored behind glass-fronted cupboards. The double sink was of shining stainless steel. It was the sort of kitchen rarely seen outside the pages of glossy magazines.

'James,' she was saying, 'had a calling well beyond that of being a policeman.'

'But he *was* a policeman . . . among other things.'

'A great policeman.'

'And he hated Foster Adams?'

'Adams was of the devil. He pandered to perversion. He worshipped only money. His so-called "insurance"!'

'"Insurance"?'

'He worshipped mammon. His vileness was a stench in the nostrils of God-fearing men. He was an evil influence upon all who came within his power.' The glint in her eyes had taken on the sheen of mild fanaticism. 'James knew him for what he was. James fought him. Opposed everything he stood for. Even prayed for him.' As she talked wheels crunched and stopped on the loose gravel of the drive. Headlights swung and cut through the near-darkness and then were switched off. She said, 'Chris is here. *He'll* tell you. *He'll* tell you how hard his father fought for the soul of Foster Adams.'

A few moments later the son joined us in the kitchen of the farmhouse. He was a man running to fat, with heavy jowls and a fast-receding hairline. He wore pebble-lensed spectacles, a fleece-lined anorak and green gumboots. We introduced ourselves, shook hands and he spoke to his mother.

'I think it's your bedtime, dear. I'll bring your hot drink up later. After Superintendent Lyle and I have had a short stroll outside.'

Outside it was chilly and I was the one without the fleece-lined anorak. I suffered and promised myself a whisky when I once more reached civilisation. Meanwhile, we talked.

He tilted his head and said, 'The stars. They're clearer here than anywhere else I know. No industrial muck to get in the way. That's why.'

'They're around,' I grunted. 'They've been around a long time. They'll still be around long after we're worm meat.'

'But beautiful.'

'Some say.'

'The moon, there. Now, why on earth does everybody want to go to the moon? Why *is* that, I wonder.'

'To check that it's not green cheese,' I suggested. 'To double check that the Man in the Moon really isn't Ben Gunn.'

'You have a sense of humour, superintendent.' He lowered his eyes to a more earthly level and stared at me through the gathering darkness. He added, 'That's something Father lacked.'

'Nor is your mother a prolonged belly laugh.'

'She's a very religious woman.'

'Is that what it is?'

'My father too.'

'I know. He was a lay preacher.'

'Would you believe . . .' He chuckled softly. 'All that gospel talk, and they have an agnostic for a son.'

'I believe most things,' I assured him. 'With a little proof of course.'

'Of course.'

'Tell me about Adams,' I suggested. 'Foster Adams.'

'Father could have talked for hours.'

'About Adams?'

'For hours,' he repeated.

'*I* don't believe in Spiritualism,' I said. 'I don't expect your father to answer. That's why I'm asking you.'

'I pay him protection money,' he said calmly.

'Really?'

'He calls it "insurance". "Protective Insurance" – that's what *he* calls it.'

'What do *you* call it?'

'I call it a reasonable price to pay.'

'For what?'

'This land.' He removed a hand from its pocket of the anorak long enough to make a quick, but all-embracing gesture. 'A few thousand acres. It's one of those geological conjuring tricks. Out here, surrounded by heather, and there's a few thousand acres of good pasture land. Arable is out. Too many rabbits. But, I've built up a good herd. Pedigree shorthorns, and one of the best breeding bulls in the north.'

'A farmer who doesn't own his land,' I mocked gently.

'Oh, no! I own it. I own every blade of grass and every beast that feeds on that grass. And I'm a *good* farmer.' He'd met my mild sarcasm head on. 'I was never much good at anything else. No scholar. No academic. But I had a flair for livestock. And Father was wise enough to know. Show me a hundred beasts, and I'll tell you which is best for breeding. Which will give the best milk yield. I have an eye for these things.'

'And you pay Adams . . . er . . . "insurance"?'

'Lyle, I don't give a damn—'

'*Mister* Lyle,' I snapped. 'Or, if you prefer it, *Superintendent* Lyle.'

'You can go to the devil.' He matched tone for tone. 'I call nobody "mister" on my own land.'

'You will,' I promised. 'Eventually. Meanwhile, you were expounding the virtues of blackmail.'

'Insurance.'

'If the other word offends you.'

'Lyle, I carry pedigree stock. The best that money can buy. All it needs is anthrax. All it needs is foot and mouth. The bugs are available, if you know where to get them. There are a dozen diseases, any of which could put me in a bankruptcy court.'

'And the bugs?' I teased. 'Adams knows where to get his hands on them?'

'What do you think?'

'I think you're a damn fool,' I said bluntly. 'I think you're a frightened little man, despite all your wind and piss. I think Adams has you in his vest pocket and that, periodically, he takes you out to check you're still ticking. Since you ask . . . *that's* what *I* think.'

26

Back at the Eagle Arms I had a stiff drink, ordered late dinner then took the lift up to my room for a hot soak and a change of linen. I was down to string vest and Y-fronts when the telephone bell brought me back into the bedroom.

The switchboard girl said, 'You're through, caller,' and almost immediately Adams's voice exploded, 'What the hell's going on?'

'And who the hell is *that*?' I put barbs in my voice too, as I made believe not to recognise the man at the other end.

101

'Adams. Foster Adams. I want to know what the devil—'

'Adams,' I rapped, 'you have just slipped off your pony. I've left the bath running. I'll be back when I've turned the taps off. Meanwhile, remount and try cantering before you break into a gallop.'

I dropped the receiver on to the bedside table with enough force to make his eardrum jerk, wandered back into the bathroom, turned off the taps, returned to the bedroom and picked up the phone.

'Now then . . .' I began coldly.

'I'm sorry, Superintendent Lyle.' Even over the wire, the apology was like a fish-bone lodged in his throat. He continued, 'I shouldn't have gone off at half-cock like that but, hell, there's a uniformed clown outside my place . . .'

'The Blue Boar?'

'He's going crazy. Christ! He's already cost me a small fortune in lost custom.'

'What's he doing?' I smiled at the duvet as I spoke. 'Cartwheels? Handstands? Backflips?'

'Superintendent, I'm serious.'

'Okay. What *is* he doing?'

'Dammit, he won't let them park within a hundred yards of here. No yellow lines, nothing like that, just that they're causing an "obstruction" . . . that's what *he* says. He's checking driving licences. Insurance. Road tax. Jesus Christ! He's checking *tyres*. For a certain fact, I know he's issued three summons reports. The man's lost his marbles.'

'He's uniform,' I said solemnly. My smile had broadened into a grin.

'I know that. He thinks that glorified monkey suit gives him the right to—'

'*I'm* CID.'

'Hell, you carry the rank, don't you? You should be able to do *something*.'

'I'm new to this force.'

'Hell's teeth! Are you telling me that *you*, a superintendent, can't chop this crazy flatfoot down to some sort of size?'

'There's a superintendent – no, a chief superintendent – in charge of City Division. I'll have a word with him.'

'Clarke?'

'That's the chap. Chief Superintendent Clarke.'

'He's an arrogant idiot.'

'He might listen. Fellow officers . . . that sort of thing.'

'Do your best, Lyle . . . please.' The last word was something of an afterthought.

'Of course.'

'I can – y'know – show my appreciation.'

'I'm sure.'

'And will.'

'I'm sure you will.'

'Good luck, old man. And thanks.'

'Rest assured,' I lied, 'I'll do my best.'

I returned the receiver to its rest, waited a moment, then asked for an outside line. Headquarters gave me Clarke's home number and within a couple of minutes I was talking to the boss man of City Division. He was obviously a man with little doubt about his own importance.

'Lyle? Who the hell's "Lyle"?'

'Detective Superintendent. The man who's taken Calladine's place.'

'Oh! *That* Lyle.'

'I'd like a word with you, Chief Superintendent.'

'Obviously. That's why you've telephoned.'

'Have dinner with me this evening,' I suggested.

'Eh?'

'Nine o'clock, at the Eagle Arms.'

'Why the devil *should* I?'

'To get acquainted. Because I seek advice. Because they serve excellent food. I could come up with a dozen more reasons if those aren't enough.'

'Are you being funny, Lyle?'

'Chief Superintendent,' I said, solemnly, 'I was never more serious in my life. You'll do me a personal favour if you'll dine with me this evening.'

'There has to be a reason for this call.' He sounded suspicious.

'A good reason,' I assured him.

'To get acquainted? Because you want advice? Because they serve good food at the Eagle Arms? Come off it, Lyle. I didn't arrive with this morning's laundry.'

'A reason,' I insisted. 'A *good* reason.'

'And that is?'

'A reason that has to be explained face to face. Not over a telephone wire.'

'Lyle.' There was a distant sigh in his voice. 'I have had a very rough day . . .'

'I'm sorry.'

' . . . I've lost my temper and taken some of the excess steam out on my wife . . .'

'She'll understand.'

' . . . and now, she's sulking like a spoiled child. And the hell she'll understand.'

'Bring her along,' I suggested.

'It's *not* police business then?'

'It's police business,' I assured him. 'But it won't take long. We can discuss it while she's powdering her nose.'

'Lyle.' There was another and deeper sigh. 'You intrigue me, son. I've a damn good mind to accept your invitation . . . just to see exactly what makes your wheels go round.'

'Please. Eight forty-five for nine? I'll meet you both in the lounge for a pre-dinner drink?'

There was a moment's hesitation, then he said, 'You're on.

And be warned. My wife *always* chooses the most expensive items on the menu . . . especially when she's recovering from a bout of the mopes.'

27

I'd helped myself to a generous portion of the hotel's 'hospitality' foam bath cream and now I was soaking gently in hot water and suds and allowing my thoughts to become as airy as the bubbles.

I was, of course, being taken for a ride.

I didn't yet know how, or in which direction, or even by whom, but I could recognise rails when I was being pushed along them. Just that I *was* being taken for a well-oiled ride.

The Blue Boar, for example. No better, no worse, than a few thousand clip-joints scattered around this fair land of ours. Gambling for your delight or whores for the asking. Booze by the bucketful, if that was all you needed. You could even *eat* there . . . after a fashion. A strip show, a few coloured lights and an electric organ with drum accompaniment.

Big deal!

What in hell was so naughty about the Blue Boar? Why the hands raised in horror? Photographs of what it had to offer were there at the entrance. The damn place couldn't even run to a car park.

Okay, if it tended to make the noses of some of the less broadminded of Lessford's citizenry tilt, that was no problem. A touch of harassment . . . as was happening at this very moment. People who frequent such dumps drive motor cars and once they are behind the steering wheel, any copper who feels so disposed can grab a fistful of short and curlies.

It can be done. It should have been done – assuming everybody was telling an unvarnished yarn – and it had not needed a newly arrived detective superintendent to work *that* one out.

At any time since its opening, the Blue Boar could have been closed within a month.

Foster Adams?

In the first place, he was no Charlie Richardson. He was no Reginald or Ronald Kray. From a provincial point of view, he was no Stafford and he was no Luvaglio. Coppers who know their onions will tell you. The truly *hard* men of crime do not surround themselves with objets d'art . . . mainly because they couldn't tell Chippendale from chipboard. They are the bish-bash-wallop boys. They eat caviare because caviare is expensive – they eat it to prove they can *afford* to eat it – but their real taste stops short at beans on toast. Their arguments begin and end with the thick stick and the open razor. The booze they drink has to damn near melt dentures, otherwise it is a 'cissy' drink.

Adams was not of that mould and yet, from the information fed to me, he *should* have been. Okay, maybe there are exceptions to the general rule and maybe Adams was one of those exceptions . . . but only maybe.

But Adams, and things appertaining to Adams, was only part of the mystery. This was my third day as detective superintendent and, other than the three murder files I'd rooted out for myself, nobody had hinted that Lessfordites committed crime. I was there, primarily, to nose out whoever was playing hare-and-hounds, but that (according to Gilliant) was something nobody else in the force knew about. To Sugden, to every other copper in the area, I was a simple, up-and-down jack. I carried rank and I had certain responsibilities. The files were still on my desk, but my in-tray didn't yet hold so much as a paper-clip.

Detective superintendents do not draw their salary as easily as *that*. Not even detective superintendents still wet behind the ears.

The murders? Ah yes . . . the *murders*.

Before my time, of course, but only just. I'd read the files and, to an extent, I'd asked around. No more than that, but the thing was still very much off centre.

Major crimes, you understand. Murder no less. And these were *files – police* files – which meant they should have included tentative conclusions, educated guesses, informed opinions and the like. What they were was a collection of bald and quite useless facts. Statements, reports, forensic science data . . . period. Not a hint of who might be responsible. Not the ghost of a suggestion of possible motive. They were a trio of sterile collections of useless gunge. So much waste paper.

Detective Sergeant Wilkins? A character suffering the name Jean Baptiste. A hard-nosed, slightly gun-happy cop and a professional killer. That on the face of things, but Wilkins tended to act like something from the Continental Op. era and 'mechanics' couldn't be found at many street corners.

As the water in the bath slowly cooled I grew more and more suspicious. I was, it seemed, a patsy. Fine! But while I *knew* I was a patsy I had the edge. How *much* of a patsy – who was playing footsie with me, and who wasn't – didn't matter too much. The trick was to daub everybody as a liar.

28

Clarke was one of those goons who favour a Kojak hairstyle. Nor was it alopecia; eyebrows Mephistopheles would have been proud of and a yard-brush moustache ruled out any ailment which might have brought on baldness. This one shaved his dome whenever he shaved his face. He was thickset, turning to podgy, and within five minutes of buying them a pre-dinner drink I had him tabulated. He was straight from the box marked 'Superintendents/Chief Superintendents – Common or Garden – Not To Be Consulted When Decision Making'.

This one was unpopular with the men under his command . . . they always are. He claimed credit and refuted blame . . . they always do. The chances were he'd reached his present rank by 'knowing' people, and by not making mistakes, and he hadn't made mistakes because he'd *never* chanced his arm. And because he'd never chanced his own arm he saw no reason to cover for anybody who *did* chance his arm . . . regardless of justification or non-justification.

I knew his type well. They clutter up every force in the country, like weeds in a not-too-well-tended garden.

His wife was a tiny, birdlike woman who disposed of a bloody Mary in two quick swallows. Birdlike in appearance, but with a voice which scratched the eardrums and a laugh capable of splintering mirrors. She laughed a lot. The prospect of a free dinner had obviously improved her temper.

I kept a fixed grin in place as we worked our way through marina herrings in sour cream, roast turkey with stuffing and cranberry sauce and, of course, appropriate vegetables, fresh fruit meringue nest and whipped cream, Gaelic coffee and cheese and biscuits. We took our time, and by the time we'd killed the second bottle of wine the woman was mildly tipsy. Clarke stayed moderately sober. I made damn sure *I* stayed sober.

Clarke had been right. His wife could certainly put it away. She had two helpings of just about everything and almost three times as much wine as either her husband or I.

As the waiter refilled her coffee cup Clarke placed his napkin alongside his plate, stood up and said, 'I'm going to point Percy.'

'Eh?'

'At the porcelain,' he smiled.

'Oh?'

'Will you join me?'

'Why not?' I too stood up and we strolled from the dining room.

As we made our way along the corridor to the toilets, he growled, 'It had to be *us*, Lyle old son. That woman has a stomach like an incinerator and where her bladder should be there's a barrel. She hardly *ever* pees.'

I had, it seemed, found favour with this illiterate clown. The all-men-together talk was the way his kind sealed the bond of newly found friendship.

When we'd zipped and were washing our hands he said, 'You mentioned something about police business when you telephoned.'

'Foster Adams,' I said expressionlessly.

'Him?' He frowned. 'Again?'

'Again?' I stepped up to the hot-air dryer.

'I've had salt on my tail because of him once today. Grant gave me something of a going over.'

'Really?'

'Six beat men and a beat sergeant accepting back-handers from the Adams bastard. Grant had me in and blew his bloody top.'

'He would.'

'I damn soon sorted that lot out.' The air from his mouth was hotter than the air being blown on to his hands. 'Shifted the lot, smartish. A new sergeant and six new beat men with firm instructions. Squeeze Adams till his bloody pips squeak.'

'That's what he telephoned about,' I murmured.

'Eh?'

'Earlier. Asking favours.'

'Who? Adams?'

'Adams.' I nodded.

'Telephoned *you*?'

I nodded again.

'Why the hell *you*?'

'Ask Adams.' I moved my shoulders. 'Would I do what I could to ease the pressure?'

'Do what *you* could?'

'Clarke,' I said, patiently, 'the men are turning custom away from the Blue Boar. He wants less police aggro.'

'You know Adams, do you?' The conversation was taking a distinct turn for the worse. 'You're on friendly terms with the toe-rag?'

'We've met,' I parried.

He pulled his hands from the blower, waved them around a little and snarled, 'Good. Well, the next time you "meet", tell him he can kiss my arse.'

'He's obviously not your favourite character.'

'No. Nor are *you*, Lyle. And – something for you to sleep on – tomorrow morning I'm into Grant's office, first thing, to report this conversation.'

'And when Grant asks the obvious question?' I purred.

110

'Eh?' He glared.

'Clarke,' I snapped. 'Six men, one sergeant. That's all . . . so far. But City Division has *three* sergeants. It takes more than *one* to doctor the beat rota every day of the year. It takes more than one . . . or it takes an inspector or a chief inspector to make sure it's permanently doctored. There's a few horse droppings to be shifted from *your* stable before anybody can eat from the floor.'

'Eh!'

'Think about it.' I turned nasty. 'Give it long and careful thought, Clarke. Before you start beefing to Grant. You might find Grant will beef back, and he'll have a damn sight more muscle than *you* have. And *you* sleep on *that*.'

29

One trick to me!

I was burning both ends of the candle but I knew it. I also knew that Adams had somebody planted in the Eagle Arms. The speed with which he'd telephoned had dropped the hint and now that 'somebody' had seen Clarke and his wife dining with me and reported to the Blue Boar. I knew *that*, too. *And* that the cuckoo in the nest had a pass key.

Clarke and his not-so-good lady had departed in what the flash novelists describe as petulant indignation and, after a last whisky and water, I returned to my room. The envelope was on the bedside table.

It was sealed. It was addressed to Detective Superintendent Lyle. In the top left-hand corner were the words

PRIVATE AND CONFIDENTIAL. The name and the words had all been typed. The 'e' and the 'E' were both a little out of alignment.

I weighed it in my hand. If they were tenners I estimated something around the five hundred pound mark. If they were fivers, half that. I didn't check. I signed my name across the sealed flap and dated and timed the signature. Then I put the envelope with the invitation to dinner, pending a more secure resting place.

Before I fell asleep I took time to wonder how Faber was finding things. It didn't keep me awake. Faber would fall on his feet . . . he always did.

30

I showered, then shaved with shaving cream and throw-away razor. Of necessity I had to look at my face in the mirror and it was no great start to a new day. Much of the discoloration had gone, but the stitches did little to improve features which showed the wear and tear of a short lifetime's overwork and irregular meals. I was lucky. The ulcers hadn't yet caught up with me . . . but given time they would.

I padded back into the bedroom, dressed leisurely and as I knotted my tie wandered to the window to check the weather. The drizzle had returned. It was now a steady downpour which gave the impression of seeing the buildings across the street through frosted glass.

The city's main public library was directly across from the Eagle Arms; one of those Victorian chunks of deco-rated ugliness, with a colonnaded entrance and a flight of shallow steps. The mackintoshed figure sheltering from the weather and half hidden behind one of the stone columns was obviously waiting for me to make an appearance. I didn't hurry. Why the devil should I? I already had some of the answers I'd been brought in to seek, and the chances were I was going to be fed either moonshine or something I already knew.

Before I took the lift for the usual giant-sized breakfast, I slipped the envelope and the note into an inside pocket of my jacket. They were precious documents. Given a fair breeze and boffins capable of performing moderately good scientific comparisons of typescript I already had Adams ready for delivery on a charge of Attempted Bribery. It wasn't much, but it was *something*.

It tagged him as a mug of course. But that's what he *was* . . . and that's what he *shouldn't* have been!

I settled down to an after-breakfast cigarette, then hurried through the drizzle to the Cortina. I drove it past the front of the hotel, turned the corner by the public library and when I was out of sight of possible watchers drew in to the kerb, leaned across and unlocked the front passenger's door.

A few moments later Wilkins ducked into the car and slammed the door against the weather. He was wet. He even smelled wet. In a bad-tempered voice he remarked upon the obvious.

'I'm bloody soaked.'

'I believe you.'

'I've been waiting more than an hour.'

'I believe that too.'

'It's urgent that I talk to you, but I don't trust the switchboard people at the Eagle Arms.'

'Nor do I.' I moved the Cortina away from the kerb and into the traffic flow. 'Okay, now you've aired your verbal muscles, what's worth risking double pneumonia for?'

'They're collecting tonight at seven o'clock.'

'"They"?'

'The Adams crowd. The bully boys.'

'What, exactly are they "collecting"?'

'The rake-off. The weekly tally for protection.'

'Where?'

'Various calling points. One of them is a pub called the Bunch of Grapes. Out North End way.'

'And?'

'It's on Delaney's patch – what *used* to be his main stamping ground – and he's gathered a bunch of would-be soldiers ready to wage war.'

'On Adams's men?'

He nodded.

'Whose idea?' I asked, gently.

'Delaney wanted to—'

'Delaney couldn't think his way through a two-times-two sum, sergeant. Don't bullshit *me*.'

'All right.' He made a quick, spread-palms movement. 'Things need pushing. I dropped a hint, here and there . . . but he still thinks *he* came up with the idea.'

'Okay.' I flicked the wipers on to fast-wipe as the downpour increased. 'We'll be there. Just you and me. We'll pick up the pieces . . . meanwhile, where's your car?'

'The Odeon car park.'

I flicked the trafficator to turn right at the next junction.

'I'll drop you. Pick your car up, change into dry clothes, then I have a job for you. Force Record Office. There's an annual list of officers – divisions, sections, authorised strength and actual strength, that sort of thing – and I want a copy of that list for the last three years.'

He grunted his understanding.

'Then,' I continued, 'I want you to make an appointment with the Inland Revenue. The Inspectorate. I want a man with us tonight. Somebody who can spot Toytown names in whatever sort of books this pub keeps. If he needs a warrant, arrange that, too.'

'We're taking the Bunch of Grapes apart?' He sounded surprised.

'We're removing a brick, sergeant. One small, perhaps very insignificant, brick. Let's say it's the start of a demolition job.'

31

On the west coast the sun had scored a victory over the clouds. It wasn't yet warm but the faint taste of salt on the lips made a pleasant change from the muck I'd been breathing in at Lessford for the last few days. The sea licked the base of the promenade and the breeze from the Irish Sea felt good and homely.

I'd dropped Wilkins at his car, then I'd left Lessford and pushed the accelerator hard down and headed for my old force headquarters. I'd passed a quick hello with a handful of old colleagues, then I'd visited Malrick's office. Detective Chief Superintendent Malrick, Head of CID. I'd asked a favour, and he'd obliged. He'd been able to oblige because he'd once been an inspector in the Met and knew people in high places I didn't know.

Then I'd driven the few remaining miles to Rogate-on-Sands and been lucky enough to find the manager of the Nat West with a few minutes to spare.

'I thought you'd left us.' He'd waved me to a chair.

'Lessford.' I'd settled into the chair and taken the sealed envelope and the invitation from my pocket. 'Promotion to detective superintendent.'

'So I'd heard.'

'These.' I'd dropped the two articles on to his desk top. 'I need them to be kept safe. *Very* safe.'

'We have branches at . . .'

'I know.' I'd smiled. 'But I don't know the Lessford managers. We even have safes at the various police stations, but I don't want them left *there* either.'

'What are they?' He'd mixed interest with surprise.

'An invitation. An envelope in which I think there's a bribe . . . I haven't checked.'

'Look, Lyle, it's a little . . .'

'I know. It's "unorthodox" – "unusual" – but you have my assurance I'm not asking anybody to put his neck on the chopping block. Just that in Lessford there's a clique. There's *always* a clique – I don't have to tell *you* – but I know the members of the Rogate clique. I know the ones I can trust. You, for example.'

He'd still looked a little worried.

It had taken little more than five minutes to convince him. He was a very honest man and we knew each other. I think his hesitation had been something of a token gesture in the name of the bank itself. Then, he'd put my own envelope and the invitation into a large manila envelope, sealed it, stamped it with the bank's rubber stamp, then signed and dated the seal.

'A safe deposit box in the strong room?' he'd suggested.

'Fine.' I'd smiled my satisfaction, we'd shaken hands and I'd left.

And now I was at the prom rails. Staring out to sea, but seeing nothing. Only remembering what Malrick had told me.

'He died, almost two months ago. In a Parisian back street. Everything points to him having bitten off more than even *he* could chew. That, or he took the pitcher to the well once too often.'

Malrick had telephoned his buddy at New Scotland Yard. The buddy had been the Interpol link between

London and Paris and Paris had come up with an immediate answer. And Interpol didn't *make* those sort of mistakes.

'He's dead?' I suspect I'd sounded very surprised.

'By this time,' Malrick had grinned, 'he'll have been measured for a shovel. For sure he won't be taking harp lessons.'

That was the information I was trying to stitch into what I already knew as I watched the waves creep in to play everlasting tag with the base of the prom.

A voice said, 'Take deep breaths, old son. It's some of the best air in the world.'

I recognised the voice before I turned to greet its owner.

'Bull' Adams. At seventy plus he looked years younger and fitter than most men ten years his junior. Some years previously he'd retired from the army to live with his daughter and her husband at Rogate. He'd become bored, bought a run-down café, turned it into one of the best winery-cum-eating-houses in the district and was now one of the few truly happy men I knew.

He joined me at the rail and for a few moments we stared at a horizon as sharp edged as a knife-blade. Above us a helicopter whirred its way lazily towards the gas platforms anchored in Morecambe Bay.

'D'you like Lessford?' he asked at last.

'It's a place,' I hedged. 'A big place. Like most cities.'

'Not like here.' We were fencing with words. Gently and without malice. But he was probing and I wasn't ready to give him a straight answer ... partly because I didn't *have* a straight answer. He added, 'People from cities come here for a holiday.'

'People also go *to* cities for holidays,' I smiled.

'Not if they've any gumption.'

'London? New York?'

'They're special. There's not much special about places like Lessford.'

117

'Maybe you're right,' I conceded.

There were a few moments of quiet, then he growled, 'This is a nice place, son. Years ago, when we were chasing Rommel across North Africa, I used to dream about this place. The peace. The quiet. The *cleanliness*.'

I nodded a sort of understanding.

'Sand,' he continued and his tone had a dreamy, faraway quality. 'There's sand and *sand*, y'know. The bloody stuff we were trudging through. Not like *this* sand. It damn near choked you at times. I remember . . .'

He paused, but I made no attempt to interrupt his memories.

He continued, 'Rommel. He used that bloody sand to outsmart us more than once. He used the *sand*. Like the time we really had him on the run. No tanks . . . see? We had the Med bottled up. Musso couldn't get supplies across to him from mainland Europe. We'd knocked hell out of the Africa Korps and he just hadn't enough tanks to stand and fight. He hadn't *enough*.

'Then – suddenly – there it was just over the horizon. Clouds of bloody sand. *Clouds* of it. And in the distance the noise. Tanks! A bloody sight more tanks than *we* had. We had to stop. We had to regroup. We had to change tactics and be ready for a second Alamein.' His chuckle was appreciative of an enemy deserving of respect. 'Rommel. The crafty old bugger. He'd bolted aero engines on to trucks and sent 'em driving around, just out of sight. Bags of noise. Bloody great clouds of sand from the propellers. He'd conned us rotten and given himself time to make an organised retreat to a position of *his* choice. He was still on the run. But at *his* speed.'

'He threw sand in your eyes . . . figuratively speaking,' I said, and my gaze never left the skyline.

'That he did,' agreed Adams. 'That he bloody well *did*.'

'But only for so long.' I think my voice was too low

for Adams to hear, and he didn't reply. I repeated, 'But only for so long.'

32

Adams and Adams.

I'd driven back to Lessford and for most of the way my mind had played tag with possibilities and probabilities – with police rank and the absence of police rank – with what I already knew, what I'd been told, and what I suspected.

And, strangely, two men carrying the same surname personified part of my dilemma.

'Bull' Adams and Foster Adams. Rogate-on-Sands and Lessford. One was decent, as innocent-minded as a child, and a man I'd admired for more than a few years. The other was devious and hawked titillation, counted himself able to buy off legal irritations others had to suffer, and was responsible for the killing of at least three people. The good and the bad. That which I knew and that which I had yet to discover.

The journey had taken more than an hour and for that hour I'd worried at the problem much as a terrier worries an old slipper. I'd shaken it from side to side. I'd tossed it into the air. I'd thrown it aside, then pounced on it from another angle. I'd growled at it, snarled at it, chewed at it and sniffed at it.

It was still an old slipper. I'd unstitched it a little but there were threads I hadn't yet driven my teeth into.

I parked the Cortina and walked into Lessford Headquarters, then up the stairs to my bright and shiny office. The three murder files were still on the desk top. There was something in the in-tray. Three things. Photocopies of the annual list of Authorised Strength, Actual Strength and Section and Senior Officers, for the last three years.

I lowered myself into the desk chair, lighted a cigarette and began to glance through the photocopies. It took about three draws on the cigarette to find what I was looking for, then check and double check.

I lifted the phone from its rest, asked for Force Records Office then, when a policewoman's voice answered, I tried to unravel one more knot.

'Briggs,' I said. 'Detective Chief Superintendent Briggs.'

'What about him, sir?'

'Where is he? What's happened to him? I have the latest list of Section and Senior Officers in front of me. He's included. Where do I find him?'

'He's retired, sir. He retired just after Christmas.'

'Retired?'

'Early retirement, sir. For health reasons.'

'What sort of health reasons?'

'Something to do with the heart, I think.'

'Where's he living now?'

'The Algarve, sir. Somewhere just outside Monchique . . . that's what I'm told.'

'Good God!'

'Sir?'

'Forget it,' I sighed. 'Forget I even asked.'

I did some more telephoning, and about fifteen minutes later Wilkins was with me, making explanations and offering opinions.

'Briggs was a passenger, sir,' he said, bluntly.

'He was Head of CID.'

'That's Sugden's job really.'

'The hell it is!' I exploded. 'Any more than *my* job's *yours*. A force this size. The ACC (Crime) takes overall responsibility, but the field commander – the man on the spot – is Head of CID. And – again in a force this size – *that* carries chief superintendent rank.'

120

'Maybe *you'll* make it,' he smiled.

'Wilkins,' I said, grimly, 'I want to know *why*?'

'Why, sir?'

'Why the Head of CID suddenly retires. Why he almost immediately takes a fast boat to Portugal. Why the vacancy was never filled . . . not even by Calladine. Why a whole heap of things.' I pushed the murder files across the desk, towards him, and ended, 'And, first of all, why the blazes these files make no mention of Anthea Carter and Joseph Henry Keanan setting up home together.'

'They do.'

'The hell they do. I've read them cover to—'

'Calladine himself took the statement. I know. I was there. I witnessed it. It's a very long statement. Very detailed.'

'Find it. Show me it.'

'It's there. In the file relating to the Keanan killing. For God's sake, superintendent. A man gets knifed. One of the statements *has* to be about his common-law wife.'

'"About"?'

'*By*. The rules of the game. Next of kin . . . one of the main suspects in the initial stages.'

'Find me Carter's statement,' I insisted.

I lighted another cigarette and watched him as he thumbed his way through the Keanan file. He checked it twice, then his eyes narrowed.

'The file's been doctored,' he said.

'If the statement was ever there.'

'It was *there*. I know. I've read that bloody file a dozen times.'

'Doctored?' I said, quizzically.

'The statement's been taken out. Believe me, super-intendent. It *was* there.'

'Why take it out?'

'God knows, but—'

'Other than to destroy evidence of the connection.'

'Eh?'

'The connection – the bedroom connection, between Keanan and Carter.'

'That's crazy.'

'Crazy?'

'Everybody knew.'

'*I* didn't know.'

'You're new here. Everybody on the case knew. Everybody who *knew* them knew.'

'Calladine knew?'

'Of course. I've already said. He took the statement. I witnessed it.'

'Sugden knew?'

'I guess. Of course. He was at the briefings, some of them, and the subject was mentioned enough times. Yes, I'm sure he knew.'

'Briggs?'

'Certainly Briggs knew. He organised the inquiry, alongside Calladine.'

'So-o . . .' I drew on the cigarette, then screwed what was left of it into the ashtray. 'The file's been doctored. The relationship between Keanan and Carter isn't mentioned in the file . . . but according to you everybody *knew* about that relationship. A question, Sergeant Wilkins. Who was supposed not to *get* to know about that relationship?'

'I guess . . .' He gave a little shrug. 'The answer has to be *you*, sir.'

'The answer *has* to be me,' I agreed.

I held his gaze for a few seconds more than normal, then in a quiet voice said. 'Remember last Monday, Wilkins?'

'Monday?'

'My first day here. The two of us, here in this office. We were talking about the murders – all three murders – the knifings of Barnes and Keanan and the strangling of Carter. Remember?'

122

'Yes, sir.'

'We conversed . . . if you recall?'

'Yes, sir.'

'I asked you about the three victims. You even admitted to rather *liking* Keanan.'

'Yes, sir.'

'All that . . . but no mention of Keanan and Carter living tally.'

'I – I thought you knew. I took it for granted that you knew.'

'How the hell *could* I have known?'

'The files.' He moved his head. 'They were on the desk. I took it you'd read them.'

'I'd read them,' I admitted.

'In that case—'

'The *doctored* files.'

'Yes, sir.' He shook his head in either perplexity or mock-perplexity. 'But how was *I* to know that?'

I lighted yet one more cigarette, but didn't hold the packet out to Wilkins.

I said, 'The question arises. Who doctored the Keanan file? Who removed Carter's statement?'

'Could be anybody.'

'You . . . for example?'

'Why the hell should I—'

'But it *could* be you?'

'It *could* be me,' he admitted tightly. 'But, it bloody well *wasn't*.'

'Easy, sergeant,' I warned. 'Too much protestation . . . you know what that sometimes means.'

'It wasn't me, sir.' The words were hard and flat, and I almost believed him.

'Calladine?' I suggested.

'He could have. But why should he?'

'Sugden?'

'Again . . . why should he?'

123

'Briggs?'

'Briggs is retired. He's living—'

'I know. Somewhere in the Algarve. Out of harm's way. But – before he left – he *could* have removed the statement?'

'He had access. Of course he could. Anybody could . . . from Gilliant down.'

'From Gilliant down.' I repeated his words, then allowed the silence to lengthen until it almost quivered.

'Okay.' I weaved cigarette-smoke patterns in the air. 'The file was doctored. Next question. *Why* was it doctored?'

'It . . .' He shook his head. 'It doesn't make sense.'

'No?'

'Those who knew them knew they were living together.'

'Common knowledge . . . was it?'

'*Fairly* common.'

'By those *in* the know?'

'Ye-es. That about sums it up.'

'Then, *I* appear on the skyline and the file's doctored.'

'It's – y'know . . . suspicious.'

'It's more than suspicious,' I growled. 'It's bloody obvious. The carnal connection between Keanan and Carter was something to be tucked under the carpet.'

'If possible,' he murmured.

'If possible,' I agreed.

'But once you started stirring things up – once you asked a few questions about the undetected murders, you'd be told.'

'Would I?'

'Well, for God's sake . . .'

'Wilkins,' I interrupted, 'I found out via a particularly dumb flatfoot who wasn't even *on* the inquiry. He, too, took it for granted that I knew.'

'*I* could have told you.'

'But you *didn't*.'

'I've already explained—'

'Let's go into this Baptiste character a little,' I cut in. 'No mention of him in any of the files. But you're very sure. Right?'

'He's Adams's hatchet man, sir. Believe me.'

'And that, it would seem, is all I'm allowed to do.'

'Sir?'

'Believe *you*.'

'I was close to Adams, sir. I was close to him via his daughter.

'Caroline?'

'I made it my business to pop the odd innocent question in, here and there.'

'That makes Adams an idiot,' I said, gently.

'Sir?'

'You're a copper, Wilkins. At the time, you were a detective constable. Very ambitious . . . if my surmise is near the mark. Adams is responsible for the killing of Charlie Barnes and Joe Keanan . . .'

'And Anthea Carter.'

' . . . and others. If you're to be believed.'

'It's true, sir. He's the most evil sod—'

'He's certainly the *dumbest* sod,' I cut in. 'To take an up-and-coming plain-clothes jack and whisper those sort of secrets into his eager little ear. I don't buy it, Wilkins. I do not *buy* it. *You're* not that good. *He's* not that thick. Somebody is taking me – maybe both of us – for a ta-ta. I'm being asked to believe something I refuse to believe, and *you're* doing the asking.' I paused, then ended, 'Maybe *you're* the dumb-bell, Wilkins. Maybe you're the one who's been fed pap and been made to believe it's prime cut. Have you ever thought about *that*?'

33

Tracing the sister hadn't been any Sherlock Holmes job. I'd asked a handful of people in Carmile Street and Carmile Crescent. I'd been told the church in whose yard the Carter woman had been buried and the cleric had given me the name and address of the person who'd organised the interment.

Moyna Carter.

'She's a lecturer at one of those private colleges, superintendent.' The parson was young and innocent. Such things seemed to impress him. 'She's a very intelligent woman.'

I'd thanked him, jotted down the address then settled down for another moderately long drive. Before leaving Lessford I'd called at the local garage to have the tank filled and while the attendant had been busy a middle-aged man with a short-back-and-sides hairstyle had strolled up and introduced himself.

'Superintendent Lyle?'

I'd admitted to the name.

'Larson.' He'd contorted himself in order to shove his forearm through the half-open window to shake hands. 'Ex-inspector, motor patrol. All the Lessford lads know me. We give a good service, superintendent. Twenty-four hours a day, and none of your big-hammer mechanics. Cost price for coppers.' Then, to the youth holding the nozzle, 'The last gallon on the house, Fred.'

'Yes, Mr Larson.'

I'd twisted myself in my seat a little in order to complete the token handshake and before he'd hurried back towards the open doors of the well-equipped workshop he'd said, 'Don't forget, superintendent. Anything. Any time. For you people we guarantee a good job.'

There's one – sometimes more than one – in every police district. It isn't, strictly speaking, lickspittle. It is, mainly, a business proposition. There's a shunt-up and a smashed car needs towing away from the scene. These garage owners specialise in that sort of service, twenty-four hours of the day. The smashed car ends up in their garage, the driver wants repairs done as quickly as possible and the insurance people go through the motions.

Nobody minds. Nobody loses. The garage gives value for money and at the same time has an edge over its competitors. It isn't a fiddle and it's one of the little-talked-about perks of being a copper.

I was making for the Halifax outskirts – the muck-and-brass area of Yorkshire – where only the locals know where Halifax, Huddersfield, Cleckheaton, Heckmondwike and a dozen other similar townships begin and end. Bingley, Shipley, Pudsey, Morley . . . but I was making for Halifax. Narrow, winding roads which weaved a way between mean-looking shops and meaner-looking houses. The factories and the engineering works, the office blocks and the tatty looking recreation grounds. And the people. No longer cloth cap and muffler but, no matter what they wore, they carried the same hangdog, damn-your-eyes quality of pent-up anger.

'From Hull, Hell and Halifax, good Lord deliver us.' That's how the saying went. And Halifax with good reason. In the bad old days the rest of the United Kingdom used the gibbet and the gallows. Not so Halifax. They had their own guillotine, and not one based on the French model. A damn great blade, which wasn't particularly sharp, with a massive weight at its root to give it impact when it arrived. *And* if the victim was particularly notorious, he was beheaded face upwards. The citizens of Halifax had had a way of doing things. *Their* way.

And now I was looking for a citizen of Halifax called Moyna Carter. I hoped her ideas were a little less radical than some who had once lived here.

I was in the outskirts, where occasional piles of Edwardian architecture gave proof of the importance of the local wool barons. West of the Pennines it had been cotton. East of the Pennines it had been wool. East and west it had been sweated labour and bloody great mills, with the owners living like minor Lords of Creation in ugly, stone-built palaces. Now the gods had gone and their places had been either bulldozed to one side or converted into self-contained flats.

I was looking for one of those flats, and it took longer than I'd expected to find it.

The building still stood in its own grounds, and the grounds were still surrounded by a solid, eight-foot-high wall. The wrought-iron gates were still in place and on both sides of the wide tarmacked drive, the grass and bushes seemed to be waiting for another summer's maintenance.

I parked the Cortina at the side of the porticoed entrance then checked the list of names and bell pushes alongside a door heavy enough to bounce back a tank.

I thumbed one of the buttons and a woman's voice said, 'Yes?'

I moved my mouth a few inches closer to the grilled speaker and asked, 'Miss Moyna Carter?'

'Who is that?'

'You don't know me, Miss Carter, but I'm Detective Superintendent Lyle, from Lessford. I'd like a word with you, if you please.'

'Detective Superintendent who?'

'Lyle.'

'I don't know any Detective Superintendent Lyle.' The voice was tinny as it came from the speaker.

'I've taken over from Detective Superintendent Calladine.'

'Taken over?'

'He died – he was killed in a road accident – a few weeks ago. I've taken over his job.'

'Oh!' There was a pause, then the question, 'What is it you want to see me about?'

'Your sister. The murder of your sister.'

There was a longer pause, then, 'You have some sort of identification with you . . . have you?'

'Of course. My warrant card.'

'Right.' I heard the soft click as the electrical lock on the door turned. 'There's a lift. My place is on the first floor. First door on your right as you leave the lift. If you're who you say you are – if you'll have your warrant card ready for me to see . . .'

'Thanks.'

I pushed open the main door, rode the lift to the first floor then held my warrant card for her to examine through the peep-hole in the door of her flat.

As she opened the door for me, she said, 'Forgive me for being so careful. With Anthea having been murdered, I tend to be over suspicious, sometimes.'

'Nobody is ever over suspicious,' I smiled. 'I should have telephoned before I arrived.'

'It wouldn't have helped.' She led me into the flat. 'I've only been home about ten minutes. No more than a quarter of an hour. That's what made me a little doubtful.'

The impression of the flat was that of tidiness without being finicky. Come to that, the impression of *her* was very similar. 'Neat and clean' would have described both the flat and its occupant. There was nothing flamboyant, but there was nothing prim and proper.

She waved me to an armchair and said, 'I'm brewing

tea, if you'll excuse me for a few minutes.'

'Not at all.'

I settled into the chair and our conversation continued between kitchen and living room.

'Join me in tea and scones,' she smiled.

'Thanks.'

'Earl Grey, Darjeeling?'

'Whatever you're having.'

The living room had plenty of bookshelves and their contents looked as if they'd been read and reread. Le Carré rubbed shoulders with Shaw, and Milton was sandwiched between Kipling and H. R. F. Keating. Halliwell's *Film Guide* stood alongside Glaister's *Medical Jurisprudence and Toxicology*. Her interests were both wide and conservative, if the contents of her bookshelves were a guide.

She called, 'Smoke if you wish. I'll be having one when I join you. There's an ashtray on the hearth.' A pause, then, 'Oh, and switch the electric fire on if you feel cold.'

'I'm fine, thanks.'

I lighted a cigarette and bent forward to bring the large, glass ashtray a little nearer. There was an easiness about the place – an easiness about the way she accepted my presence – which made for relaxation. In some strange way I felt welcomed.

She joined me, carrying a tray with collapsible legs. She placed it midway between the two chairs, then sat down. The tray held two beakers of tea. Each beaker had a motto fired around its side. Mine read 'This is the first day of the rest of your life'. Hers read 'Work is the curse of the drinking classes'. The plate was piled with buttered scones. There was a sugar bowl, a milk jug and two spoons.

I glanced at the mugs, then murmured, 'I wouldn't have thought.'

'What?'

'These motto things. You don't look the type.'

'*I* didn't buy them.' She smiled. 'I have half a dozen. All presents from Anthea . . .'

130

'I'm sorry.'

'She bought them whenever they caught her eye: 'If you can't smell burning, we're having salad for lunch'. That sort of thing.'

'She had a sense of humour?'

'Of a certain kind.'

We munched buttered scone and sipped good tea as we talked. It was a slow, easy-going conversation and if it was question-and-answer it didn't move towards even token interrogation. We seemed remarkably comfortable in each other's company, and not for one moment did I doubt what she told me.

I said, 'Tell me about your sister.'

'Anthea?'

'I need to know. The file – the murder file – records the bare details. No more.'

'She was murdered . . . but of course that's why you're here.'

'Was she the sort of person you might *expect* to be murdered? By that, I mean—'

'I know what you mean, superintendent.'

'Was she?'

'Discounting mugging. Discounting her having been assaulted – raped – then murdered to stop her from identifying her attacker. Discounting *that* . . . no.' She shook her head. 'We weren't so different. She wasn't quite as serious – no, not serious, *solemn* – as I am but other than that we were very similar.'

'You're – er – "solemn"?'

'Our sense of humour differs. *Differed* . . . I'm sorry, I'm not yet used to the idea that Anthea isn't here any more.'

'What's your job?' I asked.

'Lecturer. Social Psychology.'

'Therefore . . .' I hesitated. 'Your sister wasn't as well educated as you are?'

'There's a difference.' She gave a quick, sad smile. 'Mine is knowledge . . . something than can be learned.

Hers was simple common sense ... something you're born with.'

'For somebody with "common sense" ...' I paused long enough to draw on the cigarette and sip tea. The subject was delicate but, however obliquely, the question had to be asked. I said, ' ... she did some rather foolish things.'

'I'm sorry?' She frowned puzzlement.

'Her form, her Previous Conviction form ... it's part of the murder file.'

'Her Previous Conviction form!'

'When she crossed the path of the police.'

'Superintendent, my sister was never *once* in trouble with the police.'

This time it was my turn to look puzzled.

I said, 'It's there – on the file – nothing too serious, but—'

'*Nothing.*'

'Oh!'

'Nothing at all. Not even a parking ticket. We were too close for me to ever have doubts. We had no secrets. She knew everything *I* did. I knew everything *she* did. Everything.'

'There – there must be some mistake.' I found myself stumbling over the words. 'Somebody else's – God knows how – but somebody else's PC form must have been attached to the file by mistake.' I knew damn well it *wasn't* 'somebody else's' form, but it was the best I could do on the spur of the moment. I added, 'I'll see it's removed before this evening's out.'

'I don't like it, Superintendent Lyle.' The words were calm, but very cool. 'It's not your fault ... obviously. You weren't in charge of the inquiry. But I'm not pleased.'

'Of course you're not.'

'And without making too much trouble for anybody, I'd like whoever was responsible to be told to be more careful in future.'

'You have my word on *that*,' I assured her, and meant it.

'Anthea . . .' She swallowed and blinked before continuing. 'She was – she was . . . *good*.'

What next? I reached for a scone, bit into it, chewed, swallowed, then said, 'As a favour, Miss Carter, as a personal favour to me, tell me about your sister. Tell me *about* her. Anything. Everything. What she liked. What she disliked. Tell me as much as you can – as much as you want me to know – about her life. As much as you can bring yourself to tell me.'

It could have been a boring story. One thing, for sure, it was very commonplace. Decent parents. A decent upbringing. An annual holiday at some seaside resort. A moderate education, but with the acceptance that her elder sister had the edge on brains and, of the two, would end up at university. A job as a shorthand typist. The odd affair, but nothing too serious and no hint of wedding bells.

'And that's it,' she ended. 'Nothing very exciting. Nothing worth being strangled for.' She stood up and said, 'Your beaker's empty. I'll bring the teapot.'

She hurried into the kitchen. She took longer than was necessary. I guessed she was dabbing her eyes and trying to regain some sort of composure. The telling of the tale had choked her up a little.

She returned, refilled the beakers and after we'd sugared and milked I offered her a cigarette. She took one and I held the flame of the lighter. Then, when we were both settled once more, I continued my probing.

I said, 'No mention of Keanan?'

'No.' She bit the word off, then compressed her lips.

'He, too, was murdered,' I reminded her.

'I didn't approve.' Her voice was little more than a whisper.

'Of the murder?'

'Of Anthea living with him.'

'Any particular reason?'

133

'Old-fashioned morality. He was a married man, with a family. If she *had* to have a bedmate, she could have chosen somebody without other responsibilities.'

'You didn't like him?'

'I didn't like what they were doing. Joe Keanan was no worse than a hundred other men . . . just that Anthea shouldn't have shacked up with him.'

'You had a quarrel? You and your sister?'

'No.' It was a simple answer and had the ring of a truthful answer. 'I disapproved. I told her so. But it was her life . . . it had nothing to do with *our* relationship.'

'There is a link,' I said gently. 'There *has* to be a link between the two killings.'

'Of course.' She drew on a cigarette. 'That's *your* job, superintendent. I told Calladine all I knew, but it didn't seem to amount to much.'

'And what *do* you know?'

'What I've told you. About Anthea. Like you, he listened. Like you, he said the obvious . . . that there's a link. But he never discovered the link.'

'Knowledge?' I suggested.

'I beg your pardon?'

'Something they both knew? Something somebody didn't *want* them to know? Something they had to be prevented from spreading around?'

'That sounds rather dramatic. Even melodramatic.'

'Murder,' I reminded her, 'tends to *be* "dramatic". It doesn't happen in every family. And – if you care to call them a "family" – it very rarely happens twice in so short a time.'

She nodded slowly.

'Okay.' I sipped my tea. 'You've told me about your sister. Now tell me about Keanan.'

'I didn't know him too well. Only what Anthea told me.'

'He was a small-time crook.' I corrected myself. 'I *think*

he was a small-time crook. I *think* he'd been through the police hands at various times in his life.'

'It wouldn't surprise me. I only met him a couple of times. He was smooth. Slick. I don't like the type.'

'And?'

'He worked as a croupier at the Blue Boar. I think he creamed a little off the top for himself. He as good as said so. He was the sort to make that kind of boast.'

'That,' I murmured, 'is an activity likely to be frowned upon by Foster Adams.'

'Foster Adams?'

'The proprietor of the Blue Boar.'

'Oh!'

'And other places.'

'You mean . . .'

'I don't know *what* I mean,' I admitted with a slightly theatrical sigh. 'I don't *think* I mean what *you* think I mean. The stakes aren't high enough. But if Keanan only fiddled the kitty enough to afford a place in Carmile Street, it doesn't make much sense. A beat up, maybe. His fingers broken, perhaps. But not a knife in his guts. And certainly not the companion killing of the woman he was living with.'

34

The Bunch of Grapes had been by-passed in the rush to make every drinking house slick and highly polished. It was a boozer in the old-fashioned meaning of the word. It didn't serve food. Its sole purpose was to provide beer to men and women with gullets like four-inch drainpipes. No background music, no juke-box, no one-armed-bandit, no pintable, no in-house TV. There wasn't even a piano. Just a long bar, beer pumps, tables and chairs and a dart-board nobody seemed inclined to use.

I'd left the Carter woman, having milked her dry of every ounce of information she'd been able to give about her murdered sister. I'd left with the impression that Moyna Carter was one of the most honest people I'd ever met. Right or wrong, she'd told me the truth as she knew it. No frills. No excuses. And it didn't fit.

I'd called at a kiosk and telephoned Sugden on my way back to Lessford. Then I'd met up with Wilkins, and he'd been alone.

'The tax man?' I'd asked.

'Nobody available.'

'We're talking about an income tax racket.'

'Of course.'

'You explained that to them?'

'Sure.'

'And, they're "short-staffed"?'

'That's what the man said.'

I'd sniffed disgust before growling, 'Okay, we do it two-handed . . . but we *do* it.'

'Why not?' He'd looked mildly surprised.

'Why not?' I'd agreed grimly.

And now we were in the tap room of the pub, awaiting developments. It was a smoky, smelly dump and at 7.30 p.m. the evening business of serious drinking hadn't yet got under way. We sipped at pint glasses of bitter – half pint measures would have made us look poofters in this company – and muttered inconsequentialities as we waited for something to happen.

'I thought these bloody places went out with Hogarth,' I murmured.

'Very Dickensian,' grinned Wilkins.

Other than a trio of men huddled around a table in the far corner of the room, we were the only customers.

136

The trio were grumbling amongst themselves; their talk was bespattered with betting jargon.

'What the hell's a "back-to-back-double"?' I muttered.

'Why?'

'Those three.' I jerked my head slightly. 'Whatever it is, it seems to be deserving of an uncommonly long discussion. They seem to be finding bugger-all else worth talking about.'

'Betting-shop mathematics.'

'Hell's teeth!'

'The one in the bibbed overalls . . .' I glanced round, then nodded. 'A cowboy joiner. He'll undercut every other builder in Lessford.'

'Is that a fact?'

'Every inch of wood – every nail, every screw – has been knocked off from some site.'

'Does he get much trade?'

'More than he can handle, but he couldn't put two pieces of Lego together without the risk of them falling apart.'

'And we *know* that?'

'Some of us know it.'

'And that the material he uses is all knock?'

'All knock,' agreed Wilkins cheerfully.

'Then, why the hell haven't we—'

'Can *you* tell one piece of wood from another? One nail from another? One screw from another?' The knowing grin came and went. 'Anyway, Adams gets a piece of the action.'

'Adams? Again?'

'He arranges for the stuff to be lifted, then takes part of the profit.'

'Coming, going, up and down,' I observed drily.

'And inside and out. Adams has this town stitched up.'

Some of the stitches were starting to take the strain, but I didn't mention that point to Wilkins.

137

There was a silence, then Wilkins murmured, 'The heavily built bastard. The one with the sweatshirt and tattooed arms.'

'I noticed.'

'A convicted paedophile. A hard man.'

'With kids?' I sneered.

'Watch him, if he joins in. Keep your groin well away from his knee.'

'This place,' I observed. 'It seems to cater for real class.'

'That counter' – the grin did its coming-and-going trick again – 'it takes more than a thousand quid each weekend.'

'Where there's muck . . .' I quoted sourly.

I tasted my beer and, as I lowered the glass, two newcomers entered the tap room. One was a cocky little runt; a pint-sized version of Humphrey Bogart complete with trench coat with the belt tied in a knot and a wide-brimmed slouch hat. He even twitched his upper lip in the approved 'Bogey' mannerism. His companion was a moderately tall man; broad shouldered and with what looked like the remains of a mouse under his left eye; his was a more casual dress of army twill trousers, open-necked shirt and jacket.

They walked up to the bar and, without having to be told, the landlord splashed neat whisky into a glass and handed it to the smaller man. He glanced at the man with the mouse under his eye but received a quick shake of the head.

'Any minute now,' murmured Wilkins.

'Delaney?' I asked quietly.

'He'll be in.'

The landlord left the bar for a back room and as he returned carrying a sealed envelope the doors burst open and Delaney and two tearaways joined the party.

'Nice timing,' observed Wilkins.

138

Delaney pointed his Beretta at the face of the miniature Bogart and snarled, '*We* collect from now on.'

The three in the corner were on their feet and the paedophile bawled, 'What the bleeding hell goes on?'

'Back off, Ruskin.' Delaney switched the aiming point of the Beretta. 'Sit down, all three of you. This is sod-all to do with *you*.'

It was good advice. The three resumed their seats.

The landlord was waving the envelope around in a very undecided way until Delaney snatched it from his fingers. At the same time one of the tearaways smashed a knuckle-dustered fist into the face of the would-be Bogart and sent him sprawling.

'That's as far as it goes.' I pushed myself to my feet and moved towards Delaney. 'You're nicked, hard man. All five of you. Put the shooter on the bar top before you *really* do some damage.'

'You can go to—'

'*Drop it, Delaney*!' Wilkins was alongside me and his Smith and Wesson was aimed at the lower part of Delaney's guts. 'Drop it,' he repeated, 'or I take your ballocks off, one at a time.'

'Hey, what the hell?'

'Your pants are around your ankles, Delaney,' I explained. 'You've been set up . . . get it?'

The tearaway with the brass knuckles rumbled, 'Who are these guys anyway?' His brain was at least ninety seconds behind the rest of the world and he suffered from perpetual jet lag. 'Delaney, you told us it was gonna be . . .'

'The Filth,' sneered Delaney. 'The Filth . . . who else?'

'And,' added Wilkins, 'we aren't yet even stained. The gun on the counter, the knuckles alongside it, otherwise this thing I have in my hand starts going "bang".'

At which point the uniformed crowd arrived.

Sugden had chosen with care. The inspector topped the

139

six-foot mark, his uniform fitted perfectly, he wore leather gloves and even carried his cane of office. He strolled into the room, glanced around then pointed with his cane. The sergeant and five coppers who were with him didn't need any further instructions.

'The van's outside, superintendent,' he said, quietly.

'Good.' I nodded. 'Delaney and his two gorillas. The gun – the Beretta – and the knuckles. Frisk them. They'll have other toys.'

'Yes, sir.' He waved his cane and three of the uniformed coppers went into action.

'The man with the bleeding mouth and the trench coat. He, too, might have some interesting objects in his pockets.'

'Yes, sir.' The cane moved again and the uniformed sergeant stepped smartly towards the Humphrey Bogart lookalike.

'Those three.' I nodded at the gaping trio. 'We need them as witnesses.'

'Yes, sir.'

'And this one.' I motioned towards Wilkins.

'What the devil—'

'Sergeant,' I said, wearily, 'since when was it illegal for some jerk like Delaney to shove a Beretta into somebody's face but okay for a detective sergeant to play similar games with a revolver? Don't be *too* bloody stupid. Give the gun to the nice, polite little wooden-top.'

Wilkins looked quite startled. Then, with a slightly sickly smile, he handed the revolver to one of the uniformed men and, more in hope than expectation, I think, said, 'The motions, of course.'

'Keep hoping,' I said flatly.

I spoke to the inspector as I moved towards the man with the mouse under his eye.

I said, 'I'll bounce this beauty outside while you start working on the landlord. Scare the hell out of him.'

140

'Yes, sir.'

'We need a detailed statement from *him* to zip everything up neatly.'

'Leave it to me, sir.'

I put an arm lock on the 'mouse' man and rapped, 'Let's join your buddies, friend.'

Out on the pavement I relaxed the arm lock, bent forward and whispered, 'On your way. Tell him what's happened, and tell him I'll see him at the Blue Boar at about midnight.'

The man snarled, 'You bastard.'

'Aren't I just? Now, run for it.'

He jumped away from me and begun to sprint down the road. One of the spare coppers was climbing from the van and made as if to chase after him.

'Leave it!' I snapped. 'He's going back to his lord and master. Let him go. The Opposition might as well know we've declared war.'

'Yes, sir.' The copper grinned open delight at the prospect.

35

Sugden was waiting at his office and Sugden was in a nasty mood. I didn't blame him. On the other hand, I didn't give much of a damn. Assistant Chief Constables tend to blow super-heated steam whenever somebody even sneezes without written permission and Sugden was no exception to that rule. Maybe he expected me to genuflect. If so, he was disappointed.

'What in hell's name are you up to, Lyle?' he bawled.

'What I'm here for.' Without being invited I lowered myself into the chair reserved for important visitors. 'What I was brought in for,' I expounded.

'Damn it! You're a detective superintendent. You're here to organise the detection of crime in the—'

'Crap.'

'Eh?' Without much difficulty it might have been possible to hang coats on his protruding eyeballs.

'Come off the boil, Sugden,' I snapped. 'I haven't *seen* any documentation about crime since I arrived. I haven't even *heard* about crime. I'm here to clean the shit from the doorstep of this force. *Then*, having done that, and assuming I can *do* that, I'll be allowed to move sideways a few notches and take up the job of run-of-the-mill detective superintendent.'

'You're out of line, Lyle,' he shouted. 'You're way, *way* out of line. And, when Gilliant arrives back—'

'When Gilliant arrives back,' I interrupted, 'Foster Adams will have been reduced to the status of dirty-postcard hawker and the bite will have been removed from everybody at present paying protection money.'

'A-ah!' It was a little like steam escaping from the blown rivet of a boiler. It certainly reduced the pressure. He treated himself to a couple of deep breaths then, in a less deafening tone, said, 'All right. I'm waiting. Or is what you've done a state secret?'

'For starters . . .' I opened a packet of cigarettes and lighted one. ' . . . for starters, I've pulled the pavement bashers who worked at the Blue Boar out of Adams's pocket. I've shifted those who were on the take. Adams now knows that we can hit the nightly take at his clip-joint. We can hit it hard enough to make him feel the pain where it hurts . . . in his pocket. Clarke is no longer a member of my fan club . . .'

'Clarke's a complete prat.'

' . . . and Grant felt part of the draught.'

'Grant doesn't know up from down. Never did.'

'Whereas *you* . . .' I drew on the cigarette. 'You know exactly what goes on in the plain-clothes branch of this region.'

'You'd better believe that, Lyle. I make it my business.'

'About Wilkins,' I suggested. 'About a certain Detective Sergeant Wilkins.'

'He's a good, hardworking jack.'

'Is he?'

'A bit hard-nosed . . . but that's no fault.'

'He carries nippers . . .'

'It's been known. Other people do. They're handy, sometimes.'

' . . . non-official ratchet handcuffs . . .'

'For Christ's sake, Lyle. Come in out of the rain. Standard handcuffs can be a bloody . . .'

' . . . *and* a loaded .38 Smith and Wesson revolver . . .'

' . . . nuisance when the man—' He stopped and gawped in mid-sentence.

' . . . with which, this evening, he threatened Delaney,' I ended.

Sugden closed his mouth. He closed it tightly; tight enough to make the muscles around his jaw quiver slightly. I gave him time to steady his personal boat. I smoked in silence for the space of a dozen heartbeats.

Then, in a quiet voice, I said, 'Do we now talk sense, Sugden, or are you determined to play Tom-and-Jerry games?'

'I'm not—' he choked.

'By God, you *are*,' I contradicted. 'That blasted rank you hold has addled your brain. You can't *be* wrong . . . even when you *are* wrong.'

The truth is, there's a strange feeling of sympathy mixed with embarrassment when a man like Sugden has the wind knocked out of him. He was a copper – a good copper and, if rumours were to be believed,

143

at times a great copper – and I wasn't enjoying the job I'd set myself. Somehow, I wanted to apologise . . . but there was damn-all to apologise *for*. I'd combed a few hairs and found a few ticks but, had everybody been doing what they were paid to do, the ticks wouldn't have been *there*.

I smoked a cigarette and waited.

He gave himself a few moments, then hoisted himself to his feet and, a little stiff-legged, walked out of my vision and to a wall cabinet behind my back. I heard the doors of the cabinet being opened, heard the clink of glasses and the sound of pouring liquid. I pondered upon what my next move should be.

Should I, for example, tell him that I'd given firm instructions to the uniformed sergeant, before we'd left the Bunch of Grapes?

'Court hearing tomorrow morning, inspector?'

'Yes, sir.'

'You'll be there, of course.'

'I'll be there. I'll be the prosecuting officer.'

'Good. Have a quiet word with the magistrates. No bail for Wilkins. No bail for Delaney. The others I don't give a damn about.'

'Understood, sir.'

It was part of the strategy, but I wasn't quite sure how much of that strategy I could yet tell Sugden.

He returned to the desk and placed two glasses of neat whisky on the surface before he resumed his chair.

'Calladine's ruin,' he growled. He reached for one of the glasses and raised it in a mock toast. 'Let's drink to Calladine's ruin.'

Before I raised the second glass in the toast I said, 'I thought he was a Holy Joe.'

'When they fall . . .' The smile was twisted and bitter. 'They *fall*.'

'They have a long way to drop.' I touched my lips with the whisky.

'You're here for a purpose, Lyle,' he said, and his voice was low and almost pleading.

'A purpose,' I agreed.

'*What* purpose? And don't tell me "to detect crime".'

'It wouldn't be far from the truth,' I fenced.

'You're Gilliant's man.'

'Yeah.' I nodded. 'I'm answerable to Gilliant.'

'Not to *me*?'

'Sugden.' I tried to be as gentle as possible. 'I don't yet know who I can trust.'

'We're both on the same side, Lyle,' he pleaded.

'Wilkins said the same thing . . . more, or less.'

He swallowed neat whisky, then said, 'Would it help you to know that I love this bloody force. I started here, as a pavement pusher, when it was Lessford City – before it became the damn great conglomerate it is today. I worked my way up the hard way. I knew Lewis. *You* wouldn't know Lewis . . .'

'I've heard of him. A bastard, if every there was one.'

'I knew Raff.'

'Not much to be proud of. The job broke him.'

'I knew Collins.'

'The "Kingmaker" . . . if what I hear is to be believed.'

'I knew them *all*. They came, they went. They each made their mark on the force. But I'm still *here*. I *love* this bloody force.'

'I don't,' I countered flatly.

'Eh?'

'Not this force, not any force. You can love a person. You can – maybe – love a piece of music, a picture, a house . . . but even that takes some believing. You can't "love" a police force, Sugden. It has too many parts. Which means it has too many flaws. It's made up of individuals, and they aren't all perfect. It's an organisation created to do a job, and sometimes it doesn't do that job as well as it should.'

'Try me.' The two words were a low-voiced appeal.

'Wilkins?' I suggested.

'A good copper. A good thief taker. Red-necked, but he knows his job.'

'A bully boy,' I said, coldly.

'Dammit, we're *all* bully boys, when the occasion demands.'

'He *enjoys* being a bully boy.'

'Okay. To that extent I've been wrong.'

'Friendly with Adams's daughter.'

'Who?'

'Wilkins.'

'Adams doesn't *have* a daughter.'

I leaned forward to crush what was left of the cigarette into the desk ashtray in order to hide the surprise which must have shown on my face, as I growled, 'That also makes him a liar.'

'Who?'

'Wilkins . . . or *you*.'

'Why the devil should I take the trouble to lie about a thing like that?'

'Wilkins is celled up.' It wasn't necessary to answer his question. 'I've left word that bail should be opposed. I'd count it a favour if you don't countermand that instruction.'

'I'm wrong about Wilkins, too . . . am I?' The question had a hint of despair around the edges.

'*I* think you're wrong.'

'Do it your way, Lyle.' He took a deep breath. 'Gilliant brought you in to do some sort of clean-up. I don't deny the force needs something of that sort. Why we can't sweep up our own droppings is something I *can't* fathom . . .'

'I'm part of this force . . . remember?'

' . . . but Gilliant sits on high, and who am I to say him

146

nay. Do it your way. Ask the questions. I'll answer 'em.'

It was complete capitulation and I figured I knew the effort it took. It had taken me four days, but I'd achieved a victory. In effect, Sugden had relinquished his authority as Assistant Chief Constable (Crime) as far as *I* was concerned. I was 'Gilliant's man' – which was true – and therefore in a unique position.

The question I had to ask had to *be* asked, but not in the form of an interrogation. Because of what Sugden had given to *me*, I had to allow him to retain complete self-respect. It wasn't going to be easy.

'Tell me about Calladine, please,' I suggested gently.

'He was what you are. Detective superintendent.'

'Not as a policeman. As a human being,' I pressed.

'He lived his life as he saw fit. He wasn't perfect, but who is?'

'He was killed. A hit-and-run job.'

'We never traced the driver.'

'How far afield was the inquiry pushed?' I asked.

'The whole of the police district and all neighbouring forces. Not 'Express Message' – it didn't merit that – but damn near.'

'He was killed outright?'

'The post mortem showed the wheels – front and rear – had gone over his chest. Crushed to hell. He hadn't a cat's chance, even if the driver had stopped.'

'Motor Manslaughter?' I suggested.

'That's how it's recorded.'

'What time exactly?'

'Eh?' Sugden's frown showed a willingness to help, but a non-understanding of my question.

'I haven't seen the file,' I said. 'I've seen the three murder files. Barnes, Keanan and Carter. But I haven't yet seen the file on Calladine's death. I know he was killed in the early hours. But I don't know the exact time.'

'Half one. Quarter to two. About that time.'

'He was on his way home?'

Sugden nodded.

'Where *was* his home?'

'Park View.'

'And he was walking?'

Again Sugden nodded.

'Do we know why? Presumably he had a car, why wasn't he driving home?'

'He was pissed,' said Sugden, bluntly. 'At least he'd *that* much sense. He left his car in the park of the Constitutional Club. That was his nightly watering hole.'

'He liked his booze?'

Sugden grunted an affirmative.

'Did he often walk home?'

'Fairly often.'

'And yet . . .' I lighted another cigarette. 'He wasn't always a lush. His record shows that. It suggests that he was a fine copper . . . once upon a time.'

'Once upon a time,' agreed Sugden.

He lifted his glass and finished off the whisky. He glanced at my glass questioningly.

'Not for me,' I murmured.

'But for *me*.' He stood up and, once again, left my line of vision. As he refilled his glass he continued speaking. He seemed to talk more easily when I wasn't watching him. 'We joined the force at about the same time,' he said. 'Lessford City. He was a good copper. We were *both* good coppers. It was happier in those days. Easier, I suppose. The bad bastards hadn't as many pillocks arguing their corner. Not as many empty excuses. It was a game, played to set rules. Both sides knew the rules and both sides kept 'em. Easier . . . yeah, a *lot* easier.

'We enjoyed ourselves. Does that sound crazy? These days it *does* sound crazy, but it's a fact. Bobbying was a hell of a lot different in those days, and Calladine and I were both in the thick of things clearing the scum from the streets.

'Then the Jesus bug bit him.' He paused, returned to his chair, then growled, 'Sorry if that remark upsets any religious scruples you might have.'

'It doesn't,' I assured him.

'Anyway,' he continued, 'he changed. Changed for the worse as far as policing was concerned. He drew the pay and did as little as possible. He was still good enough to make his presence felt, but he lacked the old killer instinct that makes all the difference.'

He tasted his drink before going on, 'His son turned out to be a mug.'

'Christopher?'

'A complete barmpot. He hadn't the simple guts to be a full-blown tearaway, but he didn't seem to be able to stop himself from being a general bloody nuisance. Joy-riding. Taking motor cars without the owner's consent. That sort of thing. To my knowledge, Calladine covered up for him on two occasions. Fixed things. Traded on his own rank and reputation to keep the silly bugger out of trouble.

'Then he bought him this farm. Out on the Tops. At the back of beyond. It keeps him out of the way. They tell me he's making something of a go at it. I wouldn't know. For Calladine's sake, I hope so. He owes *that* – and more – to his father.'

'He's also paying protection to Adams,' I said, quietly.

'Christopher?'

I nodded.

'That,' said Sugden, 'is what I call perfect, poetic justice.'

'Why?'

'Because of what he did to his old man, years ago.'

'You don't like young Calladine . . . obviously.'

'He broke his father's heart. Dammit, he'd had two doses of clap before his twenty-first birthday. He was a wild young sod. He knew his old man would bail him out of just about everything, and that was what he always expected. A personal opinion . . . Calladine

149

turned to booze because of his son's antics. Whatever he became, it was because Christopher drove him to it.'

36

It was midnight, give or take a few minutes, when I walked through the door of the Blue Boar.

I'd left Sugden a very worried man. A worried man and a puzzled man. I'd milked him dry of everything he knew about both Calladine and Adams. In effect I'd had opinions already formed reinforced . . . but *he* hadn't known that.

As I'd made to leave his office I'd said, 'Gilliant is due back from Devon on Saturday, I think.'

'He starts duty on Monday.'

'Ah yes. But he arrives back in Lessford on Saturday?'

'Yes.'

'Saturday evening,' I'd said. 'Six o'clock. Ask him to be in his office.'

'What for?'

'The answers,' I'd said shortly.

'The "answers"? What "answers"?'

'The answers to questions he's asked . . . without actually *asking* them.'

'What the hell . . . ?'

'Just leave it at that, Mr Sugden.' I'd felt drained. Tired of squirming a way through a thicket of hints and innuendos. I'd added, 'You be there too, please.'

'Six o'clock on Saturday?'

'It's important,' I'd insisted.

'If Gilliant's there, *I'll* be there.'

'Fine.'

I'd walked from Headquarters to the Blue Boar. I'd needed the air. I'd needed the exercise. I was weary of driving from Point A to Point B, then back to Point A again. Dammit, I was *weary* . . . period.

Therefore, I'd walked. I'd passed shops and in one arcade of town-centre shops I'd noticed three in the same row. A gunsmith's, displaying shotguns, rifles, crossbows and as wicked an assortment of knives and daggers as it is possible to imagine behind the steel-mesh-covered window. A sex shop, displaying soft porn magazines and videos alongside posters of scantily dressed bimbos ready for immediate action. A building society office with its window-dressing pushing percentages and imitation bank-notes at potential customers with mouth-watering abandon.

Had I believed in signs and portents I might have nodded a quick appreciation. I hadn't, because *my* guns and knives weren't tucked away behind steel wire and burglar alarms; the slags *I* was dealing with weren't the outpourings of imagination gone mad; the money *I* was worried about could be passed over the counter of any high-street bank.

Nevertheless, despite such mental meanderings, the walk had done me good, and as I entered the Blue Boar I was ready for whatever crap Adams had waiting for me.

The bouncer had been briefed. He greeted me and guided me through the main room. On stage a fair acreage of flesh was being exposed beneath swirling blue and green lights. Leather, chains and make-believe whips were part of the act and the customers were far too busy eye-popping to notice us squirming our way between the tables towards the curtained door.

Just once the bouncer jerked his head towards the postage-stamp-sized stage and grunted, 'Top class . . . eh?'

151

'Top class *what*?' I sneered.

He looked hurt at my lack of taste and our journey to Adams's private rooms continued in silence. He led me through the double doors, then left as Adams rose from an armchair alongside the fire.

'Superintendent Lyle.' He waved a hand invitingly towards the companion chair at the other side of the fire. An inlaid coffee table stood between the chairs, and cups and a decanter of what turned out to be liqueur brandy was there waiting. 'Please join me. Charles gave me your message. I'm delighted you could find time to visit.'

'Charles' hovered around in a far corner of the room, looking slightly peeved and not at all friendly. He was the man from the Bunch of Grapes; the guy sporting the remains of a mouse under his left eye.

I accepted the invitation and lowered myself into the waiting armchair.

'Charles.' Adams made a slight finger-snapping gesture and the guy with the mouse collected a simmering percolator from an elegant hotplate and brought it, and a jug of cream, to the table.

'Black . . . Charles,' I murmured.

Then came glasses and the unstopping of the decanter.

I leaned back, crossed my legs, enjoyed good coffee and fine liqueur and waited. I accepted a proffered cigarette, held the tip in the flame of Adams's lighter and continued to wait.

'Once more I'm in your debt,' murmured Adams.

'Is that the way you see it?' I smiled.

'Of course.'

'I was doing my job. People are not allowed to run around waving loaded firearms in the faces of innocent members of the public.'

'Delaney?'

'And Sergeant Wilkins . . . who, very shortly, may be *ex*-Sergeant Wilkins.'

'A strange man,' drawled Adams.

'A man given to overreaching himself.'

'I tend to agree, superintendent.'

'He tells me,' I said, gently, 'that he was once rather taken by your daughter.'

'My daughter?' The eyebrows lifted slightly.

'Caroline. She fell from Kilnsey Crag, while rock-climbing with Wilkins. He saved her life.'

'Did he indeed?' chuckled Adams.

'Saved her life,' I repeated, 'but she was injured badly enough to be chair-bound for the rest of her life.'

'A very enterprising man, our Sergeant Wilkins.' The chuckle slowed down and became an amused smile.

'True?' I asked softly.

'I may have a daughter.' The smile remained. 'I may have more than one daughter. I may have more than one *son*. These things happen when you live my sort of life.'

'But not chair-bound?' I pressed.

'Show me her. Prove she's my child. *Then* I can answer the questions.'

We were playing gentle cat and mouse with each other, and we both knew it. The man with the mouse under his eye stood aside and scowled. He couldn't figure what the hell was going on . . . and *I* couldn't have cared less. My present task was to weave a net of words around Adams. Not to snare him – he was far too wily for *that* – but to unsettle him as much as possible. To make him feel so damned *safe* . . . and then to pull the rug from under his feet.

'Wilkins is a liar,' I sighed. 'But why *should* he lie?'

'Who knows?' Adams sipped at his liqueur. 'People lie for very strange reasons sometimes.'

'To get himself *noticed*?' I suggested.

'Noticed?'

'By me. By you.'

'Oh, *I've* noticed him.' The eyes twinkled. 'He tends to

be a very "noticeable" type . . . even for a policeman.'

'Maybe he wants to get in on the act.' I moved the conversation a notch forward.

'What "act"?'

'Part of your business activities.'

'No way.' He drew on the cigarette. 'We do many things, but male strippers isn't one of them.' There was a pause. Something else was coming, and I waited. In a very casual tone he added, 'Now *you*, for example . . .'

'As a male stripper?' I smiled.

'In an advisory capacity.'

'On soft porn?'

'I have other business interests.'

'Really?'

He performed his silent, finger-snapping routine and the guy with the mouse under the eye moved towards the table and handed him an envelope. It was a large, brown envelope and it was fat and juicy with its contents.

'This evening,' said Adams smoothly. 'You did me a favour. Delaney and one of his soldiers might have goosed up part of my insurance scheme had you not stepped in. I repay favours. *All* favours.'

'Insurance?' I mocked gently.

'Insurance,' he insisted. 'I guarantee a quiet, orderly life. Without that guarantee terrible things might happen.'

'I've heard that sort of "insurance" called other things,' I said. I tasted the coffee. 'I've even heard it called protection.'

'Let us reach a compromise.' His voice was smooth and easy. 'Let's call it "protective insurance". With a man like you as general adviser I could offer copper-bottomed certainty. We'd both make money. Quite a lot of money. All tax free.'

'Is this a proposition?' I teased.

'Take it.' He held out the envelope. 'I'm not "buying" you, Lyle. I'm "thanking" you.'

'Thanking me?' I played the surprised dumb-bell.

'For removing the inconvenience of Delaney and whatever muscle he might have.'

'Ah!' I made believe to understand, accepted the envelope and slipped it into my pocket. I added, 'And Wilkins, of course?'

'Wilkins has never been more than a mild irritant, superintendent.'

I drew on the cigarette then, very blandly, remarked, 'It could, of course, be misconstrued as a bribe.'

'For something you've already *done?*'

'For something else you might *expect* me to do, at some time in the future.'

'My *dear* Lyle.' The mock outrage was a delicious put-on. I could have admired the man for his sheer impudence.

'A down payment on my future salary as "general adviser".'

'Just the two of us,' he smiled.

'Just the three of us,' I corrected him.

'Oh, you mean Charles?' His tone was airy and dismissive. 'Charles is quite safe, superintendent. Believe me.' He gave a quick chuckle. 'If he steps out of line he has more trouble than he can handle. The assault and robbery of a detective superintendent, for example.'

'*Him?*' I turned to look at the man with the mouse under his left eye.

'He was suitably reprimanded, of course. He also made a written confession.'

'Which you hold, of course.'

'Which *you* shall have, should he misbehave in any way.'

'Good. I'm glad.' Then I continued in exactly the same quiet, conversational tone, 'Because the Frenchman's dead.'

I watched his face as I spoke the words. I watched very closely and saw the sudden glint of fear, followed by relief, before his eyes took upon a controlled look of surprise.

'The – er – Frenchman?'

'Baptiste,' I said, and I allowed my voice to harden just a shade.

'Do I know somebody called "Baptiste"?'

'Jean Baptiste,' I insisted, firmly. 'You know him. He's worked for you in the past.'

'Assuming . . .' He chose his words carefully and spoke them very deliberately. 'Assuming I *do* know – or even know *of* – somebody called Jean Baptiste. Assuming he *has* worked for me in the past. Not an admission – merely an assumption – what sort of work did he do?'

'He frightened people,' I said simply.

'How?'

'He was what the Americans call an "enforcer". A sort of super debt collector.'

'I see.' He seemed to relax a little. He leaned forward and refilled my glass with liqueur. Then he leaned back in his chair again, smiled and said, 'This conversation – this *part* of our conversation – has never taken place. You appreciate that, of course?'

I nodded and sipped liqueur brandy.

'Two to one, you see, superintendent.' He glanced across the room at its third occupant. 'Charles will bear witness that this part of our conversation is a figment of *your* imagination.'

'Even when the conversation touches upon murder?' I smiled.

'Baptiste didn't murder on *my* instructions!' The comeback was too swift – too touched with sudden outrage – to leave me in much doubt. Then he lifted his thumb from his personal panic button and in a smoother drawl added, 'If, of course, he *did* murder.'

'Wilkins says he did.'

'Ah, but we've already established that Sergeant Wilkins is a congenital liar . . . haven't we?'

156

'I suppose.' I shrugged.

'Therefore?' He drew on his cigarette and waited.

I made him believe I'd reached a decision. I said, 'I think we should stop fannying around. We both know that what you're telling me boils down to a protection racket in which you want me to play a part. That you're willing to slip me wads of banknotes if I agree and that, if I *do* agree, I can become a very rich man.'

'So far,' he nodded. 'So far we can see eye to eye. I would have preferred a little finesse – a little less crudity in your choice of words – but I find no flaw in your basic understanding.'

'Extortion under threats and menaces,' I said, softly. 'That is the flash – the "official" – terminology. Is that better?'

'Rather like calling a rat catcher a "rodent exterminator",' he murmured.

'Threats. Menaces.' I moved a shoulder. 'They're no good unless they're carried out. If somebody calls your bluff and you back down, you're out of business.'

'Quite.'

'And the final threat *has* to be a six-foot hole in the ground.'

'Logic insists,' he agreed.

'Which brings us back to Jean Baptiste.'

'And?'

'He isn't around any more. Somebody could use cold steel better than *he* could.'

'Should I send a wreath?' he mocked.

'Would you know *where* to send it?'

'It worries you, superintendent.' He squashed out his cigarette, then sipped coffee then liqueur. He leaned back and continued, 'This Marseilles knife-man. He was never unique. In that particular city they can be found in every street-corner café. For money . . . *anything*.'

'You talk as if from experience,' I smiled.

157

'Why not? We're partners. We have no secrets from each other. Since you accepted that envelope – since you tucked it safely away in your pocket, with Charles as witness – we've been very much—'

'Ah, yes. Charles,' I interrupted. I did the finger-snapping trick and the man with the mouse under his eye stepped nearer. I said, 'Charles. Check the door, please.'

Charles snarled, 'Up yours, Lyle,' but he obediently checked that the door was both locked and bolted.

Adams looked puzzled, and began, 'Look, what the hell . . . ?'

'Then telephone Lessford Headquarters.' I was still talking to 'Charles'. 'Get Sugden's office. He'll have a warrant and a raiding party ready by this time. Tell him the goose is cooked and waiting for collection.'

'Lyle, what the devil are you trying to . . . ?'

'You're nicked, Adams,' I said amiably.

'I'm *what*?'

'Nicked. Under arrest. You've had your collar firmly felt.' The man with the mouse under his eye was busy with the telephone. I continued, 'You are banged up. You have the right – of course – to remain silent. But at a guess, you've said more than enough already.'

'Charles, what the blazes does this bloody detective—'

'Ah yes. "Charles".' It seemed a pity to waste good liqueur brandy. I leaned forward and topped my glass as I continued. 'To you he's "Charles". To *me* he's "Faber" – Detective Inspector Faber . . . and he never *was* on your side.'

'Dammit, he's the hooligan who—'

'Mugged me? Robbed me?' I touched my forehead. 'I'm prepared to forgive him an excess of zeal if he has what I think he has. Evidence which, alongside mine, should blast you into outer space.'

I watched Adams as he deliberately absorbed the shock of what I'd said. I admired him at that moment. It took him maybe half a dozen breaths, no more, and then he was the calm suave guy he'd been when he'd figured himself top dog. He, too, filled his glass with liqueur before he spoke. He raised his glass in a gentle, mocking toast before he held it to his lips.

'I like you, Lyle,' he said, at last. 'Damnation, I *like* you. Between us, we could have taken this town apart, stitch by stitch.'

'You're not a hard man,' I said gently. 'That, I think, was the first giveaway.'

'So obvious?' His grin was very wry.

'Adams,' I said, 'you may be a past master on titillation. You may know just about all there is to know about porn. But when it comes to hard-centred tough nuts, you're not even in the first heat. Delaney could have eaten you for breakfast.'

'That, I suppose, is an inverted compliment,' he smiled.

'Yeah.' I nodded. 'It goes with Demanding Money with Menaces, Accomplice to Murder, Attempting to Bribe a Police Officer and anything else Faber and Sugden can come up with.' I returned the smile, 'You badly need a solicitor, Adams.'

'Worry not, Lyle my friend.' He gave the impression of not being in the least fazed. 'The minute your colleagues come through the door of the Blue Boar, he'll be contacted. He'll be in the interview room before *I* am.'

37

It was past three o'clock in the morning when I slammed open the cell door and set about Wilkins.

I'd left Faber with Sugden and the truth was, Sugden

had been very shaken. That was okay. Now I *could* trust Sugden. The raid had been a blinder and the warrant he'd obtained from some tame JP covered just about everything all the way down to spitting on the pavement.

'This one?' Sugden had gawped. 'The tearaway responsible for thieving your wallet? For sending you to hospital? One of *us*?'

'One of us,' I'd insisted.

'Holy hell!'

'It's his case,' I'd continued. 'He's our main witness and he'll show you where the evidence is.'

'And don't think I won't enjoy myself,' Faber had growled. 'I had seven shades of shit knocked out of me when I sought refuge in this clip-joint. *And* I had to take it without much of a murmur.'

'You did a good job, inspector,' I'd said.

Faber had glared, then snarled, 'I owe you one, Lyle. I owe you a beaut . . . and don't think I won't remember.'

'You'll remember.' I'd shrugged. 'That's why it had to be you.'

'Why the hell should his memory—' Sugden had begun.

'He has a kinky mind.' I'd allowed myself a slightly wicked grin at Faber's discomforture. 'He remembers *everything*. He sees something, hears something, and it sticks. However important. However trivial. In the witness box, he'll give you the time and date Adams changed his socks . . . *and* what colour they were. He'll quote, verbatim, every word he's heard. Take it from me, Sugden. I've seen this character in action under cross-examination. Adams is stitched up, top and bottom.'

'Good God!'

'That's why it's *his* case. All we do is play back-up.'

'If you say so.'

'More than that, I *insist*.'

Thereafter, the police machine had gone into overdrive and the necessary books, documents and personnel had been ferried from the Blue Boar to Lessford Headquarters.

I'd mentioned the previous backhander, the first invitation and the typewriter with the off-centre 'e'.

'I'll have them here,' I'd promised.

'Do we need them?' Sugden had sounded overconfident.

'We need *everything*. We need as many dabs as we can find. We need the scientific boys to check with the gum on the envelopes for genetic fingerprinting. We need the glass and the cup Adams used for comparison spittle.'

'Oh, very technical!' Sugden hadn't been able to hold back the slight sneer.

'Sugden!' I'd rounded on him. I'd had enough and my nerves were like jagged glass. I'd rasped, 'Stay with the bull's-eye lanterns, if you must. Blow your bloody police whistle, if it amuses you. But don't kid yourself. That fancy rank you hold isn't going to bring Adams out in a muck sweat. He'll have a QC capable of eating you as a slight hors d'oeuvre to his breakfast cornflakes unless his client is nailed with as much modern know-how as we can come up with.' I paused to allow my impatience to quieten, then I'd added, 'Sugden, it's the way it's done, these days. It's no longer enough to con an admission out of 'em . . . and anyway, with Adams you *couldn't*. This one needs *proof*. We have it. For Christ's sake, let's *use* it.'

At which point I'd left a shaken Sugden, walked to the headquarters car park, collected the Cortina and driven to the North End nick.

And now I'd awakened Wilkins from his fitful slumber and was in the exact mood to give him warmed-up hell, if that was the way he wanted to play things.

He hoisted himself from the cell bed, stifled a yawn, then grunted, 'All right, Lyle. What sort of game is it you're playing?'

'The rank,' I snapped, 'is superintendent . . .'

'What the . . .?'

' . . . and the "game" is chopping stroppy young detective sergeants off at the knee-caps.'

He started to lower himself into a sitting position on the edge of the cell bed, and I rapped, 'Stand up when a senior officer talks to you, Wilkins.'

'What!'

'You may fancy yourself as an undisciplined young sod but at this moment you're in no position to demonstrate your independence.'

'Why the . . .?'

'*Stand up*. Stand to attention.'

He stood up. He stood to attention, or as near to 'attention' as he was able considering that, as per normal procedure, the belt from his trousers had been taken away and he was in his stockinged feet. He kept his knees together and nipped the sides of his pants between his finger and thumb. That's as near as he could get to 'attention'.

'You are,' I pointed out coldly, 'in police custody. Let's understand *that*, for a start. This is no "pretence". You hawked a loaded revolver around in a public place. You pointed it at Delaney and you had your finger on the trigger. *That* of itself puts you firmly up shit creek, and you're going to stay there until you've answered a few questions.'

He mumbled, 'Yes, sir,' and I knew the starch was leaving him, fast.

'Questions,' I said, 'about doctored murder files.'

'Sir, I—'

'The Keanan file.'

'Oh!'

'The Carter file.'

'Sir, I've already explained—'

'The hell you have.'

'When you said there should have been a statement from—'

162

'I'm *now* talking about Previous Conviction lists.'

'Oh!'

'Not something that's been taken out. Something that's been slipped *in*.'

'I – I don't know—'

'Carter's previous form.'

'She was—'

'She was *nothing*, sergeant. The file says she was a tart, but the file's wrong. She was a silly young bitch – she lived tally with Keanan – but that's *all* she did.'

'Is it? I didn't—'

'You bloody well *did*. You checked the files. Both files. You checked them very carefully in my presence . . . remember?'

'Yes, sir,' he breathed.

'Keanan's file . . . a statement removed. Carter's file . . . a false Previous Conviction list inserted. Doctored to hell, Wilkins. Why?'

'I – I don't know.' But he was lying, and it showed.

'She was a brainless young woman,' I said.

'Yes, sir.'

'Not a criminal. Just a brainless bint who set up home with a criminal.'

'Yes, sir.'

'Yes, sir?' I sneered. 'Then why in hell is your signature alongside her arrest for taking on paying punters?'

He didn't answer, because there wasn't a reasonable answer.

'Two murder files,' I snarled. 'Both of them doctored. By you.'

'Sir, I didn't—'

'You damn well *did*. Your signature – your initials – they're scrawled all over the infernal files.'

'I – I didn't—'

'Jesus wept!' I was shouting a little. 'You're a licked man. You're smashed. I don't need any fancy "verbals".

163

It's there, in black and white. Your signature. Your initials. More flaming lies – stupid, pointless lies – than the parson preached about. I'm not pulling blinders. I'm talking to a man who, supposedly, knows the way things work. For God's sake, come clean and salvage what little you can from this blasted shambles. Let me at least be able to say you—'

'I didn't do it for the reason you *think* I did it!'

It was like a verbal explosion. What the hell it meant, it had to be true because no man could come up with that much sincerity without it being the real thing. He was trembling a little, and it wasn't with fear. It was with emotion. Other than the slight shakes, he stood as rigid as a towbar and stared at a spot just above my head. He was no longer the cocky young detective sergeant I'd come to dislike. There was enough don't-give-a-damn pride there to stop me in my tracks and make me wonder what the hell I'd missed.

'I didn't . . .' He swallowed, steadied his voice then, still staring at the point above my head, repeated, 'Sir, I didn't do it for the reason you think I did.'

I waved a hand and growled, 'Sit down, sergeant. Let's forget why *I* think you did it. Let's be hearing why you *did* do it.'

'Adams.' He remained on his feet.

'Adams is inside,' I sighed. 'He's taken the first step towards a long session of slopping out in some prison.'

'Thank God.'

'So?'

'Baptiste.'

'Baptiste is dead. He's already rotting. He met a better knife-man than he was, sometime between the murder of Keanan and the murder of Carter.'

'You're sure?'

'Interpol don't make those sort of mistakes.'

'Thank God,' he repeated. Then, 'Thank *God*!'

Then slowly, a little shakily, he lowered himself into a sitting position on the cell bed. He held his skull between his hands, with his elbows resting on his knees, and his fingers seemed to be trying to squeeze the bone tightly enough to prevent what was going on inside from working loose. The trembling increased slightly and his bowed shoulders moved a little as he fought back the tears.

I gave him time enough to regain some degree of control, then I sat down alongside him, opened a packet of cigarettes and held it out.

'Take one,' I advised. 'For the moment we aren't sergeant and superintendent. We're two coppers. We're alone, and there's something I need to know. At a guess, something you need to tell. On the record, off the record – either – we'll decide which, later.'

He raised his head, rubbed his eyes with the heels of his hands, then sniffed.

As he accepted the cigarette, he muttered, 'You're better than most, Mr Lyle. Thanks.'

'I want the truth,' I warned as I held a match, first to his cigarette then to my own. 'I don't give a damn how hard it is – how long it takes – the truth ... or nothing.'

'The truth.' He inhaled cigarette smoke, then began, 'The truth is I tried to con you. I tried to make you think you *needed* me. I was smart-arse. Too smart-arse for my own good.'

'From the beginning,' I suggested.

He took a deep breath, then said, 'My old man – my father – God he was proud of this force. He was detective sergeant at North End – this division – under Sullivan. Hamilton – Sergeant Hamilton—'

'I've met Sergeant Hamilton.'

'Ask him. Ask *him* about my old man. About the old days, when I was only a kid and listened to how the *real* coppers handled the tearaways and the twisters. I tell you – I swear – I couldn't wait to get into the force. *This* force. I wanted to work alongside the old man. To be as good as *he* was. Maybe to work under Sullivan or, if not Sullivan, somebody as good as Sullivan.'

He paused to take a couple of inhalations of the cigarette. I could have asked a few questions, but it would have been foolish to do so. The man was reliving part of his past and, in so doing, hinting at answers to some highly charged questions.

'The Adamses. I knew them both. The old man and Foster. My father used to tell me. Delaney could be handled. All *he* had was muscle. Even as a young tearaway he could be dumped without too much trouble. But old man Adams had the cunning. He was slippery, and his son learned the trick. Slippery. Know the right people. Grease the right palms. It can be done. It could be done in the old days, and it can still be done. That's why my old man retired without once feeling Adams's collar. It was the one thing he regretted. His one failure . . . as he saw things.

'He only lived two years after retirement – I'm talking about my father – but by that time I'd bunked myself up to detective constable. I tried to take over where he'd left off – my father, I mean. He was a damn good jack – one of the old school – and he passed on all the tricks he knew. He even introduced me to some of his informants. We'd talk, after he'd retired, we'd talk about the old days and the way things were changing. The usual "bobby talk". And Adams always cropped up. How he might be nailed. How he *should* be nailed. How he'd grown to be the big cat who could never get caught. Foster Adams. The local porn king. The creep every crook in the city was scared of. The protection racket he'd built up. The whole damn city, and how he was gradually slipping it into his hip pocket. Including the force. *Our* force. *My* force.'

166

The passion was coming through. A passion bordering upon religious fervour. Too much passion – far too much self-involvement – for a working copper. Here was another who "loved" the police service, and it was getting in the way of that cold objectivity necessary to do the job properly. It was the reason -- and, to him, reason enough – for a brand of hellbent lunacy which, already, had landed him inside a police cell. If it wasn't curbed it would turn against him and become a club his enemies could use with which to beat out what few brains he had left in his skull.

He smoked in silence for a moment, then continued.

'I didn't know who to trust. That's what it boiled down to. Other men in the force. Who was, and who wasn't, taking backhanders. It was a one-man mission. It *had* to be. Just me, against Adams. Me, and bastards I had firmly by the balls. It got so I couldn't trust fellow coppers. The detective inspector – I don't know for certain, I still don't know for certain – but he *could* be on the take. I knew about Briggs.' He paused long enough to take a single draw on the cigarette. 'Charlie Barnes slipped me the wink about Briggs. The bloody Head of CID. I mean, if you can't trust *him*, who the hell *can* you trust? Barnes was one of Adams's heavies – when he wasn't thumping people for his own amusement. I had him . . . see? A particularly nasty GBH. It could have been blown up to Unlawful Wounding without much effort. Maybe even Attempted Murder. The bastard he'd done over wouldn't have been a great loss if he'd gone all the way, but Charlie Barnes was firmly in the frame and I did a deal with him. I'd stay dumb and leave the file open in exchange for griff about Adams. Something to nail the big man with. The old sprat to catch a mackerel gag. That's about all he came up with. That Briggs – our illustrious Detective Chief Superintendent Briggs – was on the take in a big way. It made me careful. It made me *very* careful. I mean . . . if Briggs was in on the nawpings who the hell *wasn't?*'

'Calladine?' I suggested gently.

I figured it was time I said something. Wilkins was starting to thrash around in deep water and I didn't want him to get the sudden idea that he might drown. I wanted him up on the surface until *I* decided whether or not to push his head under the waves.

'Calladine!' The contempt made his voice ugly. 'Did you ever *meet* Calladine?'

'No.'

'A real "come-to-Jesus" prat.' The half-grin showed absolute contempt. 'That one. He wasn't interested in slamming the sods behind bars. He wanted to "save" 'em all. Sugden's buddy and between them they pussy-footed around Adams and *allowed* him to be cock o' the midden. They *allowed* him to get on top – and to stay there.'

'Backhanders?'

'I don't know. If Briggs was taking the grease, who *wasn't?*'

He smoked his way through another slice of bitter-filled silence before he took up the story once more.

'Barnes was knifed, of course. He was mouthy. The chances are he mouthed a little too much and Adams took him out of circulation. Adams . . . via Baptiste. I didn't feel like contributing to a wreath. It didn't matter too much anyway. By that time I'd worked my way close enough to Keanan. I didn't need Barnes. Keanan worked at the tables in the Blue Boar. He knew more than Barnes would ever know. He had brains. More brains than Barnes ever had. He tipped me off about Baptiste. How the Frenchman was brought over to do the killings. I learned a lot from Keanan. A hell of a lot. And, the more I learned the more I realised that nobody – *nobody!* – could be trusted.'

'Not even Keanan,' I observed softly.

168

'He must have talked. Dropped a hint to somebody who mentioned things to Adams. The Frenchman dealt with *him* too. That was the jungle I was into. Dangerous. *Bloody* dangerous.'

He dropped what was left of the cigarette on to the concrete floor of the cell and I screwed what was left of the glowing tobacco into black ash before I spoke.

I said, 'The doctored files?' I made my tone friendly, but with what I hoped was the right degree of puzzlement.

'To get at you before Adams did.'

'Explanations, please,' I pressed gently.

'Look . . .' He waved his arms slightly as he sought the right words. 'I needed somebody. Somebody with rank. Somebody I could trust. Somebody I knew damn well wasn't under Adams's thumb. You were new. From another force. You were taking over from Calladine. That meant you'd be taking over the murder inquiries. You'd be looking for a link. Something the others might have missed. Okay – I fiddled the files and made *myself* the link. That's all. To get at you first.'

'Why not just walk into my office and say your piece?'

'Would you have believed me?'

'I'd have listened.'

'Then asked questions. Verified that I wasn't a complete nutcase.'

'Probably,' I agreed.

'Told the wrong guy. Unknowingly, you'd have passed the word to Adams.'

'Wilkins,' I said, wearily, 'the whole bloody force isn't rotten. Every apple in the barrel isn't rotten. Or . . .' I smiled, 'maybe you *are* a nutcase.'

'You don't believe that, sir. Not now.'

'I believe you're a liar,' I said. 'All that crap about saving Adams's daughter's life. That was . . .'

'That was stupid,' he admitted, heavily. 'That was meant

to make you believe that I *knew*. That I wasn't spinning fairy tales. That I'd been close enough *to* know.'

'You have a very vivid imagination, sergeant.'

'I didn't imagine what happened at the Bunch of Grapes, sir. That was real enough. You were there. You saw it. The weekly graft was handed over to Adams's men.'

'Before Delaney crowded it.'

'To let you know that even a tearaway like Delaney hides behind a gun when Adams calls the tune.'

'You, too, needed a gun,' I reminded him. 'It's why you're here.'

'Sir, I'm scared.' The heavy sigh which accompanied the admission was real enough. 'At this moment, I'm shitting myself. I don't know what I've started. I don't know how it'll end up. You say Baptiste is dead, but there are other "Baptistes" around, and if Adams crawls from under . . .'

'He won't.'

'I'm scared,' he repeated, and I believed him.

I stood up, dropped what was left of my own cigarette on to the cell floor and heeled it out.

I said, 'Sweet dreams, sergeant. You're a very accomplished liar but for the moment that's about the only point we're in agreement on. If, this time, you *aren't* lying . . .'

38

Friday. Traditionally bath day – or bath night if you go in for perfection. Maybe because I didn't want to let the side down, maybe because, subconsciously, I was an old-fashioned traditionalist, or maybe because I was just plain knackered, I was enjoying a bath. My timing was all to hell, of course. The pewter-dull light of an April dawn gave the pebbled glass of the window the hue of watered-down milk, but the hotel served its customers well and the water was good and hot, even at that hour, so I soaked my weary bones in sudded water and gradually relaxed.

I'd left word at North End Divisional Headquarters.

'Wilkins. When it gets to a civilised hour, bail him to Headquarters at six o'clock on Saturday. Tell him he's suspended from duty until he hears otherwise.'

'Sir, our last orders were—' The office duty sergeant had looked perplexed.

'I know what you last orders were.' I think I'd sounded both terse and tired. I *was* tired and maybe that had made me terse. 'I *gave* those orders,' I explained. 'They aren't embedded in reinforced concrete. I can retract them.'

'Yes, sir.'

'Six o'clock. Saturday. Headquarters. And he's to stay put until he receives further instructions from me.'

'Yes, sir.' The sergeant had seemed satisfied. He'd made a note on a slip of paper and slipped the note under the clip holding one of the files.

I slipped a little further down into the warmth of the water and idled my mind along trying to figure out a man like Wilkins.

A prat with an overactive imagination? A creep who'd read too many Hank-Janson-style blood-and-thunders? Okay, men like Baptiste *did* lurk in the shadows – but not in *every* shadow. Adams? Adams was as bent as a crummock, he was the local porn king, he ran something of a protection racket in the town, he knew people with influence. All these things, but he wasn't God! Nor, come to that, was he the son of Old Nick. A good swift kick up the arse and friend Adams would vacate Cloud Nine tout de suite.

Then why, in hell's teeth, hadn't Wilkins realised these simple truths?

171

In the luxury of my foam-topped delight I tooled around with philosopical baubles. That there was enthusiasm. That there was overenthusiasm. That there was fanaticism. Then, way up top, there was whatever ailment Wilkins suffered from. Adams's father had put a few over on Wilkins's father, ergo Wilkins had long ago lost all sense of proportion and wouldn't rest in his grave until he'd smashed Adams into individual atoms.

It was a form of lunacy, and it was a form of lunacy the force could do without. Fortunately, I wasn't solely responsible for Wilkins's future. That responsibility was one of the things Gilliant was paid to carry and, come six o'clock tomorrow evening, the burden of that responsibility would be slapped squarely across Gilliant's shoulders . . . by me.

I allowed myself a quiet, secret, but rather self-satisfied smile. Come six o'clock tomorrow evening, I was going to enjoy myself in a mildly perverted way.

Eventually the bath water cooled and I climbed out and rubbed decent circulation into my body via a couple of very expensive towels, then padded into the bedroom and phoned the night porter.

'Have the kitchen staff arrived yet?' I asked.

'Some have, sir.'

'Coffee and toast?' I suggested. 'I'll be away before the official breakfast time starts.'

'Oh, I don't know about that, sir.' He sounded distinctly doubtful.

'This rather plush hotel . . .' I said pleasantly. 'Are you suggesting its service to guests falls well short of some grubby little all-night café on some A-class road?'

'Good Lord, no, sir.'

'No?'

'Leave it to me, sir. I'll be back to you in a few minutes.'

'Do that,' I encouraged.

That was the mood I was in. A strange mood. Slightly

argumentative but not ill-tempered. I figured I'd just about ironed the kinks out; that twenty-four hours, or there-abouts, simmering on the back burner pending the arrival home of Gilliant would make everything tender, tasty and ready for serving. Sugden and Faber would be busy most of the day, interviewing people, collecting evidence and generally building a case against Adams and his cronies. I, personally, didn't want the job. I'd have been under their feet and anyway, I knew Faber well enough to be sure he'd stitch the whole thing up all the tighter without me, if only to prove what a whizz-kid detective he was. He was welcome to any medals likely to be given out.

Me? I'd asked too many questions and been told too many lies. I wanted a breather. I wanted to forget the damn job Gilliant had foisted on to me, if only for a few hours. For the moment I wanted *out*.

I fished new underclothes, socks and a shirt from the drawers and placed them on the bed, ready. I returned to the bathroom and was busy with the hair dryer when the telephone rang.

The night porter's voice said, 'Mr Lyle?'

'Speaking.'

'Your breakfast, sir. Coffee, toast and marmalade. Grilled kippers, perhaps?'

'That would be rather nice.'

'I'll let the kitchen know, sir. There'll be a corner table waiting for you when you come down.'

'Thanks a lot.'

I dropped the receiver back on to its rest, dressed with as much leisure as I required, then took the lift down to the dining room. It was unusual – pleasantly unusual – to have the echoing room to myself. Soft-footed waitresses hurried about their business, setting tables and making sure chairs and napkins were in their proper place. One waitress had been detailed to keep *me* supplied and the coffee was strong and hot, the kippers grilled to perfection and the bread lightly toasted and still warm.

I was even given a choice.

'The marmalade, sir. Orange, lemon or grapefruit?'

'Lemon, I think.'

'Yes, sir.'

I dawdled over the meal. I allowed that 'second wind' known to every working copper who's spent a night away from his bed to gradually take over. The tiredness goes. The desire for sleep melts away and, if anything, the mind takes on a strange new edge.

As I rose from the table the normal early risers were wandering into the room, sitting at tables and opening their morning newspapers as they awaited the attention of the various waitresses.

I left the hotel, walked to the car park and climbed into the Cortina. I eased the car into a road still free of its normal weight of traffic and made for the edge of town. I drove at a very moderate speed and less than an hour later I was well into the Pennines, between Skipton and Gisburn, heading west.

I was, I realised, reaching decisions. Not hurried decisions. Very deliberate and carefully thought out decisions.

I was sure I knew all the answers. Answers to questions I hadn't even been *asked*. Enough answers to satisfy Gilliant, and too many answers to satisfy me.

The answers were no problem. The problem was a couple of unasked *questions*!

I filled up with petrol at a roadside garage and, at the next lay-by, pulled in, left the car and lighted a cigarette. The few days since I'd last seen the endless zig-zag of drystone walls seemed to be an age. The slow, grass-grown dips and rises of the Pennines. The distant, isolated farmsteads, with no apparent means of access or egress. The skyscape of layers of clouds, each layer moving at a different pace from its fellows. The flocks of sheep, each flock bunched together like a huge, po-faced family; the isolated trees permanently bent away from the prevailing wind; the distant hills and beyond them, more hills, and beyond *them* and in the hazy, purple distance, even more hills.

'The Backbone of England' they called it. It was, too. It had bred dynasties of monarchs. It was a hundred times more important – a thousand times more impressive – than all the Lessfords in the world. I found myself secretly envying the copper whose beat encompassed these acres.

I stayed there until I'd finished the cigarette, and a few minutes longer. I breathed good, clean air, then walked back to the car and continued my journey.

I called in at my old force headquarters, exchanged chat with men I'd worked with for many years, then called in at the chief constable's office before continuing my journey to Rogate-on-Sands. There I called at the bank and retrieved the envelope and invitation I'd left.

I parked the car at the Rogate DHQ car park, then walked to the promenade and watched the sea. The tide was out but in the distance white horses danced on top of the waves before they spent themselves in creeping scallops along the edge of the beach.

My last call before lunch was at the estate agent's office where I'd arranged for my flat to be sold. Then to a neat little restaurant and a meal of lemon sole which had been landed at Fleetwood that same morning. Nostalgia was the name of the game and I played it for the rest of the day. Rock Walk, the pier, along the prom as far as the sandhills, then a slow stroll back to the centre of the town. My town. My people. A place of mildly amusing superiority whose inhabitants counted themselves slightly better class than others who lived on the west coast. But good people, and people I'd grown to know and respect.

I called in at the Park Theatre to watch the local amateur operatic society putting the finishing touches to their latest offering. The G. and S. masterpiece *The Yeomen of the Guard*. A slightly portly Jack Point died of unrequited love on Tower Green while a somewhat gawky Elsie Maynard embraced an equally ungainly Colonel Fairfax.

From the front stalls the producer yelled, 'Look, Madge, we're on final dress rehearsal tonight. *Please*! Kiss him as if you mean it. Your husband won't mind. He's right behind you in the chorus, and if you *do* look as if you're going too far, he has a bloody great sword handy to prod you with.'

Madge glared and snapped, 'That's not funny, Desmond.'

'It's not meant to be funny, dear. This is a very tragic story. At the moment it *isn't* tragic . . . it's *pathetic*.'

They were still bickering when I left.

It was dark when I pointed the Cortina away from the sea and started back towards Lessford. Again I drove at a moderate speed, parked in a corner of the Eagle Arms car park, enjoyed a last double whisky with ice then took the lift up to my room.

I slept like a child.

39

Sugden's mood was like a honed blade. That was fine by me. I had the stone capable of blunting it when the time arrived.

Gilliant looked as if he *needed* a holiday rather than having just had one. He sat behind his desk and smoked cigarettes. He looked worried. Very worried. Maybe he realised he had reason to be worried.

The tiny bruise under Faber's left eye seemed to have become less, but it was still slightly discoloured. He, too, looked cross, but above all he looked tired.

It was *exactly* six o'clock when I entered the office.

Sugden very pointedly consulted his wrist-watch.

'We've been waiting here for—' he began.

'Six o'clock,' I interrupted.

Gilliant gave a tiny cough and raised one of his hands a few inches from the desk top. He was still top dog and it was his way of intimating that he wanted the meeting to at least *start* with some degree of tranquillity.

Sugden compressed his lips, but kept his opinions to himself.

I'd collected the three murder files, and Wilkins, from the front office. I'd left Wilkins sitting in the anteroom to Gilliant's office. I dropped the files on to the desk, then took Adams's invitation and the packet I'd collected from the Rogate-on-Sands bank manager from my pocket and placed them alongside the files.

'Cash for an attempted bribe,' I explained. 'And an invitation to the Blue Boar, signed by Adams. Finger-prints – normal and genetic – should link them. There's also a typewriter link.' There was an empty chair, and as I lowered myself into it I asked, 'Are they *really* needed? Or have you unearthed enough?'

'We have him by the short hairs.' Faber answered the question. He sounded quite pleased with himself. 'We have the books. Names, places, amounts . . . everything. It was big enough to need documentation. That was its weak link.'

'We could have done with your help,' grunted Sugden.

'I've been busy,' I said, airily.

'Doing what?'

'Thinking,' I smiled. 'Reaching certain conclusions.'

177

'We didn't need you.' Faber cut in, before Sugden could continue his gripes. He grinned and added, 'We've had a ball. Porn and protection. Christ! It pays a bloody sight better than policing.'

'What doesn't?' I smiled.

'The Blue Boar,' continued Faber. 'That was just the front office. Blue films. Stag-party porn. Massage parlours. Brothels. A sweet little call-girl set-up. You name it, Adams could provide it . . . and did. And a regular pay-off from scores of lunatics who wanted a quiet life. You wouldn't *believe*.'

'I'd believe,' I murmured.

'Superintendent Lyle.' Gilliant spoke for the first time. 'The outward signs suggest that you've dug very deeply. That – presumably – is why we're here. To be shown the various "treasures" you've unearthed.'

I nodded, leaned forward and lifted the top file from the desk.

'Charles Barnes,' I began. 'Late resident of Gordon Court. A tearaway. No great loss to the community. A typical "enforcer" employed by a protection racketeer.'

'We know all that,' grunted Sugden.

'Do you also know he was the snout of a certain Detective Sergeant Wilkins? That Wilkins had – still has – a pathological hatred of Adams? That he put the bite on Barnes in order to collect evidence – *any* evidence – against Adams and what Adams was up to?'

'I know Wilkins.'

'Good. He's in the outer office, ready – even eager – to back every word I say.'

'If that's all you've—'

'Barnes was knifed.' I wouldn't allow Sugden the floor. It was all mine, now. It was the reason for this meeting, and the likes and dislikes of Sugden weren't important. 'He was knifed by an expert. An *imported* expert. Jean Baptiste. Baptiste was—'

178

'For Christ's sake!' Sugden wouldn't be silenced. 'If that's all you can tell us, you're wasting your time. The man doesn't exist. He's a figment of—'

'There's a phone there,' I jerked my head as I snapped my interruption. 'Get on to Scotland Yard. Contact the Interpol officer there. Tell *him* Jean Baptiste is – or was – the figment of somebody's imagination. Tell *him* he never existed.'

'We've checked,' growled Sugden. 'We aren't bloody stupid.'

'*Who* checked? You . . . personally?'

'Your damned office checked. Wilkins sent a confidential memo. It was crap. It was—'

'Baptiste murdered Barnes,' I snapped. 'You can sort out your personal incompetences later, but for the moment *I* hold the floor, and what you've just said goes a long way towards proving the point.'

'I'm damned if I see—'

'Mr Sugden.' Gilliant raised a hand once more. His voice was a little strained as he said, 'Mr Lyle is right. *He* holds the floor.'

I gave a tiny nod of thanks, rubbed Sugden's nose in the dirt by repeating, 'Baptiste killed Barnes.' As I reached for the second file I continued, 'It didn't matter much, because by that time Wilkins had cultivated Keanan. Joseph Henry Keanan. He was much closer to Adams than Barnes had been. He worked at the Blue Boar. Again, Wilkins's snout, but with a slight difference. They were almost friends. It happens sometimes – a copper and a crook, on opposite sides but they get on well together. Keanan kept his eyes and his ears open, and fed information to Wilkins. A lot of information. Enough to frighten Wilkins out of his wits . . .'

'What few he has,' muttered Sugden.

'. . . enough to produce an educated guess. Briggs was in on it, of course.'

Sugden closed his mouth very tightly. Gilliant lighted another cigarette.

Faber asked, 'Who's Briggs?'

'Detective Chief Superintendent Briggs, inspector.' I spelled it out for him, and for the other two. 'Head of this force CID. He took early retirement. Fairly recently. He bogged off to the Algarve. Somewhere near Monchique. He's neither been seen nor heard from since. In short, he did a quick bunk. The kitchen was getting too hot. He was on the slush-fund list. That's one reason murders in this neck of the woods tend to remain unsolved.'

'Wilkins?' Faber asked the question.

'At a guess.' I nodded. 'What isn't a guess is that Wilkins had dug deep enough not to know who the hell he *could* trust. And most of what he knew came from Keanan.' I flicked the second file with a finger-tip, and ended, 'Therefore, exit Keanan . . . via Baptiste.'

'Baptiste . . . *again*?' Sugden's lip curled.

'Baptiste was no bogey man.' My voice had become harsh – almost a snarl – as I fought to get the truth across to this pig-headed assistant chief constable. 'They *are* around, they *do* exist – these killers. Ask your chief constable. Of the four of us, *he* knows the truth of the matter. They're "available". If you have the money and the contacts, they're *there*.'

'They exist, Mr Sugden.' Gilliant came down on my side. In a very sombre, but very assured tone he added, 'Let's waste no more time dodging *that* issue. Barnes and Keanan were murdered by the same man. A knife expert. Accept that his name was Jean Baptiste.' Then, to me, 'Go on, Mr Lyle.'

'This file.' I flicked the file again. 'It's been tampered with. Will you accept *that*, Mr Sugden?'

'Not just on your say-so.'

'Okay.' I was going to have to fight every inch of the way. I'd half expected it. I said, 'A murder file. Other than the crime being undetected, not a particularly unique murder file. Do we agree on *that* point?'

'Yes.'

'You've read it, presumably?'

'I've studied it carefully . . . a damn sight more than "read" it.'

'There's a statement from the woman, Carter, is there?'

'Of course.'

'The usual, mildly negative statement?'

'They have to be taken.'

'In which she says she was the live-in lover of Keanan?'

'She uses the expression "common-law" wife.'

'But she doesn't know who killed him?'

'That's what she claims.'

'Or why he was killed?'

'She *says* she doesn't know.'

'About herself?' I pressed. 'The normal patter? That she was a good little girl? That she'd never been in trouble with the police? That's she'd have married Keanan, had he not already *been* married?'

'Lyle.' He was getting angry again. 'It's a very uncomplicated file. It was a very uncomplicated inquiry. A man gets himself murdered. First suspect – his next of kin. The wife. Even his common-law wife. We didn't come up with this morning's grass, Lyle. A very full – very comprehensive – statement was taken from Carter. It was necessary, for elimination purposes. Dammit, if you don't know *that*—'

'Show me the statement.'

I held out the file and everybody watched while he flipped through the pages. He flipped through twice, then a third time for luck.

He glared at me and said, '*You* didn't take it out?'

'No.'

'Then who the hell . . . ?'

'Oh, I know *who*. I also know *why*.'

'In that case . . .'

'Are we agreed that the Keanan file *has* been doctored?'

'It would seem so.'

'Hell's teeth, Sugden!' I exploded. 'It wouldn't just "seem so". It *has*.'

'All right,' he growled. 'It has. But why?'

'Because . . .' I leaned forward, then took the third file from the desk. 'Because, without doctoring the Keanan file – without removing Carter's statement – doctoring Carter's own file would have been a waste of time.'

'The *Carter* file?' Sugden's eyes began to pop a little.

'Carter,' I repeated. 'Little Miss Frilly Panties. Sweet and spice and all things nice. That's what *her* statement claims. But according to the Previous Conviction sheet in *this* file – in the file covering her own murder – she was the biggest whore since Messalina.'

I slipped the Previous Conviction sheet from the Carter file and handed it across.

'Why?' croaked Sugden. 'For Christ's sake *why*?'

'To link his name with all three victims.'

'*Who*?'

'Wilkins.' Then, as a hint of disbelief began to dawn on Sugden's face, I added, 'He's admitted it. I'm not guessing, Sugden. Wilkins doctored both files in order to get his name noticed.'

'I'll – I'll—'

'Sugden!' I was wearying of this man's refusal to accept the truth. I, too, had a temper and I'd held it in check far too long. I snarled, 'For Christ's sake open the door and come out of your own private little closet. Wilkins was taught policing by his father, and his father policed under men capable of taming present-day louts before breakfast. It may not be the "modern" way, but it's a damn *good* way. His old man was after Adams. All his life he was after Adams. Wilkins merely took up the torch.

'But who the hell could he trust? Who the hell *could*

he trust? His own boss – the Head of his own CID – was taking grease. If *he* was . . . anybody! Maybe you. Maybe his chief constable. Dammit, the only man he could wholly trust was himself.

'Then, I came on the scene. New. Somebody Adams hadn't yet had time to get at. I was the best bet. I was the *only* bet. But it had to be done in a back-door manner. Don't knock on the door and splurt it all out. That way, I'd ask around. Check that Wilkins himself wasn't some brand of nutcase. Make things a little different. Fiddle the files a little. Make *me* come to *him*. That's all he did, and that's why he did it. A frightened man, with an axe to grind and a hatred that was eating its way into his guts.

'Get with it, Sugden. Vacate that bloody ivory tower you've lived in for too long. We're talking about a man on a personal crusade. A man who doesn't give a damn *how* it's done, as long as it *gets* done.'

I closed my mouth, and Faber murmured, 'That's my boy. That's Lyle with the throttle open.'

'Cut it, Faber,' I growled.

Gilliant drummed the desk top with his fingers and, in a deceptively calm tone, said, 'Let us, therefore, retire. The canteen is still open. We'll have tea, coffee – assimilate what has been said – and cool off a little.'

40

I found myself delivering a mini-lecture on parlour psychology. I didn't like it, because it wasn't necessary and I'd once admired the man I was *really* talking to. I still admired him . . . but a little less, if only because he'd forced me into this ridiculous situation.

We'd collected Wilkins on the way to the canteen and while we'd sipped hot tea and coffee from plastic beakers some of the anger had spent itself. Sugden's scowl had gradually changed into a frown of concentrated worry. Faber's cockiness had quietened and Wilkins's apprehension had disappeared. Gilliant had worked the magic by refusing to allow the talk of his office to spill into the canteen. He'd steered the conversation into less controversial channels; a half-hearted discussion about television programmes and books, and the latest jet-set scandal.

And now three of us were back in Gilliant's office, and I was saying, 'A man gets religious mania and there's no telling what he'll do. He can become so "good" – so self-satisfied – that he ends up a pain in the arse. He creates his own "God". *He* decides what should be and what shouldn't be. He can disagree with everybody – Canterbury, the Pope, everybody! – and *he's* always right. They don't just talk to God – they don't just say their prayers – God talks back to *them*! They figure themselves to be divine. To have a private and personal hot line to the Almighty. Peter Sutcliffe – the Yorkshire Ripper – made just that claim. That God "spoke" to him. He wasn't the first. He won't be the last . . .'

We'd left Faber and Wilkins in the canteen. I'd introduced them, then said to Wilkins, 'Get together with the inspector. He hates Adams as much as you do. Exchange information. *All* information. Stitch the bastard up tight enough to stop him from even breathing.'

'Calladine.'

From behind my back Sugden spoke the name softly, but in a tone that made it sound obscene.

'Not Calladine.' I didn't turn, but continued the explanation. 'Calladine was no Peter Sutcliffe. That brand of megalomania breeds men like Rasputin. Evil, in the name of religion. The Inquisition . . . that sort of thing. That wasn't Calladine's madness. Somewhere – somewhere along the line – Calladine changed tracks. He threw his religion overboard and moved in the opposite direction. He went bent and – as always with his kind – he went all the way.

'At a guess, he recruited Adams. Adams was the perfect front. A porn merchant, with the ready-made facility to launder all the money Calladine could rake in. That's what the Blue Boar was. A laundry for crooked money. Money from protection. Maybe money from blackmail. The perfect partnership. Adams and his flesh business, and Calladine able to block police action aimed at closing that business down. Perfect . . .'

I stood with my hands deep in the pockets of my trousers and stared out of the windows of Gilliant's office. Gilliant had switched on the lights when we returned and the panes were like black mirrors through which I could see the stony-faced expressions of the other two. Beyond the panes I could also see the lights of Lessford city centre.

'If it *is* possible to construct rules governing the ways of criminals, it's fairly true to say that the sex crowd – other than top-class pimps – don't go in for murder. Or protection rackets, come to that. I've met Adams. He's hard . . . but, he isn't particularly violent. Baptiste? Oh yes, Baptiste was real enough. Barnes and Keanan were murdered by Baptiste. Wilkins dug deep enough to discover *that*. But *Calladine* – not Adams – imported Baptiste. He'd too much to lose. Far more than Adams. Equally, when it seemed possible – maybe probable – that Keanan had whispered pillow secrets to Carter, *she* had to go. But Baptiste wasn't available. Baptiste had met his match. And Calladine was no knife expert. But *anybody* can kill, both quickly and silently, with a ligature. But you knew that of course, didn't you. Both of you.' I turned to face them as I made the accusation. I added, 'From the beginning. From the day *you* telephoned me.' I looked

185

directly at Gilliant. 'All that crap about suggesting I apply for this job. Then – later – at Looe. It was a come-on. You wanted to know . . . both of you. Could whoever replaced Calladine fit the pieces together? Was your precious force likely to be held up as an example of how rotten senior policemen can occasionally *be*?'

I lowered myself into an empty chair, lighted a cigarette and felt sorry for them. Neither spoke. What the hell could they *say*?

I drew on the cigarette, then continued, 'Three crime files. I've been here a week, and that's all I've been shown. But, of course, very *important* crime files. The three murders which, given enough bad luck, *might* point towards Calladine. But you *had* bad luck. I met a particularly dumb patrol man . . . that was the first unlucky break. Then Wilkins. Nobody knew about Wilkins. Nobody guessed that a mere detective sergeant had been beavering away for years, gunning for Adams and, to help his cause, had messed around with files Calladine himself had overseen.'

'Don't gloat, Lyle.' This came from Sugden, and it was part threat but mostly a deep-throated plea.

'Gloat!' I doubt if my quick smile showed even a hint of humour. 'I don't gloat when a senior officer turns first racketeer, then murderer, Sugden. I don't gloat when the head of a criminal investigation department goes scurrying to the safety of the Iberian Peninsula because his own neck of the woods has become too hot to handle. I don't gloat . . . I *weep*.'

'You had luck, Mr Lyle.' Gilliant spoke for the first time. 'Or if you prefer, we had *bad* luck.'

'No.' Again, I drew on the cigarette. 'Forgive me, chief constable, you were bloody dumb. Whoever thought up this cross-eyed scheme was *dumb*. Calladine's son. His father bought him a farm. Cash down. Bought and paid for. What the hell with? Not a superintendent's pay.

Not a legacy from his own father . . . that much can be gleaned from Calladine's personal file. The kitchen of that farmhouse looks like something from *Homes and Gardens*. And – okay – Chris Calladine pays "insurance" to Adams – in effect, he was repaying his own father, but didn't know it – and *that's* about the most paper-thin cover-up anybody could come up with. The whole thing stinks. Those three files . . .' I nodded towards the files still on Gilliant's desk. ' . . . so much waste paper. So much garbage. But you had to be *sure*. You had to be convinced that they *looked* genuine. So-o . . . wheel on the sucker. Let Old Man Lyle root around a little. Let's check we haven't slipped up somewhere. Jesus Christ!' I drew on the cigarette, then again spoke directly at Gilliant. 'Down at Looe, you chuntered on about Operation Countryman. Just the right amount of outrage . . . right? Enough to put the bare possibilities of "cover-up" into my mind. What you *didn't* want, you claimed – but, in fact, what you *did*. But good enough – tight enough – to fool everybody.'

'Calladine's dead,' growled Sugden. 'It's over and done with. Drop it.'

'Drop it?' I mocked.

'Let sleeping dogs lie.'

'Superintendent Lyle.' Gilliant spoke slowly and with infinite sadness. 'You could smash this force . . . if you so wished.'

I nodded terse agreement.

'You could,' continued Gilliant, 'disgrace good men.'

'Good men?' I kept the mockery in my tone.

'Men who have had the wool pulled over their eyes. Men who have trusted other men because they were expected to trust them.' He tightened his lips for a moment, then continued, 'The gutter press would crucify us. Extremists from all sides would have a field day. We'd be ridiculed. It would take us years to re-establish our credibility. That's what you could do, superintendent. I even take the point

187

that that's what you *should* do – officially. A report to the Home Office. That's all it needs.'

'That's all,' I agreed.

'Will you?'

'It depends,' I fenced.

'Well, bugger this!' It was a growled explosion and Sugden let it out as he rose to his feet. As he walked, stiff-legged, to the door, he added, 'No more of it. This is *my* bloody force. I'll crawl to nobody who threatens to give it a bad name.'

41

Once more we were two men; back to the Looe situation, but with a difference. This time we were being honest with each other.

We were both worried. Maybe I was a touch more worried than Gilliant but if so, that was because I knew – or guessed – what he *didn't* know. We were both smoking and for a few moments we each waited for the other to say something.

Eventually, he gave a wry smile and said, 'Sugden tends to have a short fuse at times.'

'I'm sorry,' I said awkwardly.

'For what?'

'For doing what you hoped I *wouldn't* do.'

'It was a risk.' He moved his shoulders. 'We took it.'

'Adams,' I said, 'is a reasonable man.'

He waited.

I took the plunge, and continued, 'He'll do a deal. He'll meet you half way . . . maybe more than half way.'

'He's not the sort of man I do business with.'

'Have you ever met him?'

'No. He's a glorified pimp and a protection racketeer. That's enough for me.'

'*Calladine* was the protection racketeer,' I reminded him. 'Adams was merely his front man.'

'He remains a glorified pimp.'

'Strange.' I waved my cigarette, vaguely. 'I'm probably as puritanical as the next man, but I found him strangely attractive.'

'Really?'

'Honest.'

'Really?' Gilliant wasn't prepared to move his position too easily.

'I've dined with him.' I pressed on hopefully. 'At his invitation. In his private apartment at the Blue Boar.'

'That must have been quite an experience.'

'It was. He sells porn – soft and hard – any flavour you fancy . . . much as the Walls people sell ice cream. And to *him* that's all it is . . . a confection.'

'I would have used the word "perversion".'

'Gilliant.' I was tiring of all this pussy-footing around. I put steel into my tone. 'If you're anxious for this precious force of yours to be grilled over a slow fire, go ahead. Smack Adams over the head with the heaviest stick you can find. He'll retaliate. Of course he will. Calladine's name will be waved in court, on radio, on television and in every newspaper on the streets. That's what you'll do, and that's *all* you'll do. You won't stop prostitution. You won't stop skin flicks. You won't stop strip shows. You won't even *dent* what Adams is pleased to call "the commodity" he sells. And that's what he does. He *sells* it. He doesn't actively *encourage* it. On a personal level, I don't think he's too interested in it. Merely that the mugs seem determined to buy it from *somebody*, and he's businessman enough to make sure they buy it from *him*.'

189

Gilliant nodded, and I had the feeling I'd got through to him.

'He's businessman enough to do a deal,' I continued. 'And honest enough to keep his side of any bargain.'

'What sort of deal?' asked Gilliant gently.

'To keep Calladine's name out of things.'

'A whitewash job?'

'Calladine is dead . . .'

'That's what I—'

'It was a hit-and-run job.'

'I told you *that* a week ago.'

'You did,' I agreed. 'What you *didn't* tell me was that Calladine was once Sugden's buddy but today Sugden hates the very mention of Calladine. That Sugden knew where Calladine went for his booze and roughly when he left home. That Sugden knew that Calladine walked home whenever he was stewed. That there's a character called Larson – ex-motor patrol inspector who runs a garage – who would, no doubt, repair the odd dent in an assistant chief constable's car without asking too many questions.' I paused, then ended, 'You get the general drift, I hope?

Gilliant didn't answer. He stared ahead and even his eyes looked dead.

I took the envelope from my inside pocket and dropped in on to the desk.

I said, 'My resignation. I won't unscramble eggs – especially rotten eggs – even for a superintendent's pay. Some small advice, perhaps. Offer the job I'm vacating to Faber. He'll take it. He's a fine copper, even if his conscience isn't as touchy as mine. Do your deal with Adams. Wilkins? As long as Foster Adams ends up in a dock, *he'll* be satisfied.' As I turned to leave the office I ended, 'You'll live with it, Gilliant. We all have to live with a certain amount of dirt. Nobody can smell roses every day of his life . . . not even chief constables.'